Praise for *Hunter's Choice*

"Reedy's familiarity with the terrain, the culture of the outdoors, and combat breathe authenticity into the narrative. . . . For kids who, like Hunter, can't get enough of *Hatchet*."

—*Kirkus Reviews*

"[A] paean to hunting . . . notable for its verisimilitude and well-realized setting, the Idaho wilderness." —*Booklist*

"Vividly realistic passages about shooting and hunting enrich the narrative, while explorations of toxic masculine attitudes in hunting culture, fear of failure, and trauma underscore the steady action. . . . [An] emotionally satisfying read."

—*Publishers Weekly*

"Recommended for fans of hunting adventure stories."

—*School Library Journal*

HUNTER'S CHOICE

HUNTER'S CHOICE

TRENT REEDY

Norton Young Readers

*An Imprint of W. W. Norton & Company
Independent Publishers Since 1923*

For information about permission to reproduce selections from this book, write to
Permissions, W. W. Norton & Company, Inc., 500 Fifth Avenue, New York, NY 10110

For information about special discounts for bulk purchases, please contact
W. W. Norton Special Sales at specialsales@wwnorton.com or 800-233-4830

Manufacturing by Lakeside Book Company
Book design by Beth Steidle
Production manager: Beth Steidle

Library of Congress Cataloging-in-Publication Data

Names: Reedy, Trent, author.
Title: Hunter's choice / Trent Reedy.
Description: First edition. | New York, NY : Norton Young Readers, [2021] |
Audience: Ages 9–12. | Summary: Twelve-year-old Hunter Higgins has dreamed of,
and prepared for, his first hunting trip but now that he is old enough, he wonders if he
can kill an animal, especially with his long-term crush, Annette, nearby.
Identifiers: LCCN 2020041597 | ISBN 9781324011378 (hardcover) |
ISBN 9781324011385 (epub)
Subjects: CYAC: Hunting—Fiction. | Conduct of life—Fiction.
Classification: LCC PZ7.R25423 Hun 2021 | DDC [Fic]—dc23
LC record available at https://lccn.loc.gov/2020041597

ISBN 978-1-324-01997-8 pbk.

W. W. Norton & Company, Inc., 500 Fifth Avenue, New York, N.Y. 10110
www.wwnorton.com

W. W. Norton & Company Ltd., 15 Carlisle Street, London W1D 3BS

2 4 6 8 9 0 7 5 3 1

This book is dedicated to Travis Klima, a fantastic brother-in-law and a master hunter. May the largest buck always find his way to your stand. It's prime time!

HUNTER'S CHOICE

CHAPTER 1

TAPTAPTAP. "HEY, HIGGINS," KELTON FIELDING WHISPERED.
TapTapTap. "Higgins." Kelton Fielding was always tapping
Hunter's back, wanting to tell him something. It was only
October, and Hunter had already been in trouble four times from
talking to Kelton, usually when the guy couldn't resist offering
an update about his repairs to his ancient broken snowmobile.

Hunter let out a breath. Thirteen minutes and forty-five
seconds left. The clock on the classroom wall ran so slowly. Miss
Foudy sat at her desk at the front of the room filling out grades
or doing whatever she did during the afternoon work period.
Miss Foudy was cool, but she was nobody's fool and did not
allow talking during study time. Hunter leaned way back in his
seat and pretended to stretch his neck. "What?" he whispered.

"You gonna bag a deer this weekend?"

Hunter nodded. Of course he would shoot a deer this
weekend. Several guys in the sixth grade and at least half the
guys in the junior high and high school were going hunting this
weekend. Kelton knew darn well that Hunter was going hunting

too. Why did he ask the question with so much doubt in his voice?

"Mom's boyfriend says he knows about a cabin where a guy has a salt block," Kelton whispered. "Says a big ol' buck has been hanging 'round there."

"Hunting with a salt block's illegal," Hunter whispered out of the corner of his mouth.

"Ain't *our* salt block," Kelton hissed. "We take that buck, even off that guy's land, what's he gonna do? He can't complain much since he's already breaking the law."

For once, Hunter would have preferred to hear more about Kelton's junky old snowmobile. He shook his head. Using a salt block to illegally lure deer to the kill. Trespassing and hunting on someone's land without permission. Hunter had had the vague idea that Kelton Fielding's mom was dating a new guy. He seemed to remember that her last boyfriend had been kind of a jerk. This guy didn't seem much better. Hunter wasn't supposed to know anything about these kinds of things, but there weren't a lot of secrets in a little town like McCall.

"I'm going to take a four-by-four buck," Kelton said quietly. "Or something bigger."

Annette Willard, who sat at the desk in the next row over, looked up from the notebook in which she'd been writing. She flashed a cute look of forced irritation and pressed a finger to her lips.

"Sorry," Hunter whispered, glancing at her a moment longer.

Hunter was sure Annette really did want them to quiet

down so she could write, but she wasn't mean about it. More importantly, she wasn't about to shush them loud enough to draw Miss Foudy's attention.

"You ain't gonna bag no deer," Kelton whispered.

Hunter sighed. Eleven minutes and twenty-two seconds. Twenty-one. Twenty.

TapTapTap. "I'm gonna bring in a huge trophy buck. I bet you don't even pull the trigger."

"Shut it, Fielding," Hunter whispered.

"That's good advice for both you boys," Miss Foudy called from the front of the room, fixing them with that serious glare and doing that thing where she tapped her pencil on a book on her desk.

Hunter would've given real money if everybody would stop tapping. He quickly looked down at his social studies book. But not before stealing another glance at the clock.

Ten minutes and fifty-one seconds. Fifty. Forty-nine.

FOR ALL HIS EAGER ANTICIPATION OF THE END-OF-THE-day bell, Hunter didn't bolt from his desk and sprint for the door. Once he was free from the rigid control of the classroom and the weekend had officially begun, he felt no rush, no anxiety. Most of his assignments were done, so he wouldn't have to look at his schoolbooks until Sunday night. His clothes and boots were packed. His Remington 783 bolt-action rifle and plenty of 6.5 Creedmoor rounds were locked in Dad's pickup. He was ready.

The weekend of his first-ever hunt had arrived.

He just had one stop to make first. "Hey, Mom," he said entering the school library and spotting his mother behind the counter scanning some books. "Can I still check out a book? I need something to read during downtime this weekend."

"Sure," she said. "If you hurry. I'm trying to get everything shut down here."

Hunter headed for the fiction section. "No problem. I'll just grab—"

"*Hatchet?*" Mom shook her head in mock irritation. "Again? That would be at least the tenth time you've read it."

"It's a great book!"

"Yes." Mom nodded. "But I pride myself in running a library filled with hundreds of other good books. It wouldn't kill you to branch out a little."

Hunter pulled his favorite book off the shelf, enjoying the familiar library plastic over the dust jacket of the well-read hardcover. "Please? Just one more time? I promise I'll read a different book next."

She smiled and sighed. "It's your first hunt. I'll humor you. And it is a great book."

"The best," Hunter said. "Thanks, Mom."

She scanned the book. "You're welcome. Now would you get out of my library so I can close up for the weekend?" She laughed as Hunter bolted.

OUTSIDE THE SCHOOL, THE BRIGHT SUN WELCOMED everyone to freedom. A warm day for October. Hunter watched the school's Patriot Squad lowering the flag for the day. They had a whole procedure where three of them folded the flag in a perfect regulation triangle, while the others stood in a straight line. Later that night right before the football game, they'd march the American and Idaho flags out onto the fifty-yard line for the National Anthem. Hunter planned to join the Patriot Squad when he became eligible next year in seventh grade.

At the bike rack, he caught up to Yumi. "Hey, cousin, you got a new game you're gonna master this weekend?" Neither Hunter nor Yumi had any siblings, and since they were the same age, they'd grown up almost like brother and sister.

She scowled, wrapping herself tighter in the Army field jacket liner she used as a coat, hiding her new *Halo* Master Chief T-shirt. "I wish. Dad's acting all weird again." She picked at a string at the edge of a hole in her jeans. "Who knows?"

"Hey, slow it down!" Mr. Dufflin, the high school principal, called to some high school boys as they rolled toward the parking lot exit in a blue raised-up four-by-four pickup.

"This isn't NASCAR," Yumi said quietly, pulling her silver ten-speed bike from the rack.

"This isn't NASCAR!" Mr. Dufflin shouted, running his hand back over his shining bald head.

Yumi rolled her eyes. "The guy is so old. He's been high school principal here since way back before the school even had internet."

"Yeah, but I heard he's going to retire at the end of the year." Hunter pulled his smaller stunt bike out of the rack and stood for a moment on its back pegs, pulling the handlebars up to pop a wheelie.

"Come on, Higgins." Yumi shook her head. "They say that every year."

She ought to know. Yumi was tapped into pretty much everything that happened or that people said was going to happen. Her mom, Hunter's aunt Tomoko, owned and ran Wine O'Clock, a wine-tasting and -drinking place on the corner where the highway turned downtown by Payette Lake. A lot of people—locals too, not just tourists—hung out there, including Yumi, especially when the place got busy and Aunt Tomoko needed extra help.

"You going hunting?" Yumi asked.

Hunter smiled. For as long as he could remember, his family's main thing had been hunting. He'd always dreamed of being part of it, but the closest he'd come to a real hunt was listening to Grandpa Higgins, Uncle Rick, and his dad telling stories. He'd started shooting on Grandpa's firing range two years ago, and even Uncle Rick, who had qualified for an expert marksmanship shooting badge in the Army, said he was a good shot. He'd passed Idaho's hunter safety course and Dad had paid for his license and mule deer tags.

"Sure am." Hunter was proud to be able to tell her he was heading out with the men, finally old enough to really hunt. "I'm s'posed to ride to Dad's office, and we'll head straight to the lodge from there."

"I topped your high score on *Ms. Pac-Man* last night." Yumi mounted her bike, flashing Hunter a condescending smile.

Hunter sighed. "You did not! Come on, Yumi! It took me forever to get that score."

The ice-cream shop next door to Wine O'Clock had a back room with a pool table and an antique video game arcade. About a year ago, she and Hunter started seriously battling each other for high scores on *Centipede*, *Donkey Kong*, *Galaga*, and *Ms. Pac-Man*.

"Come on down and drop in a quarter before you go to your dad's office. Let's see what you got," Yumi said.

He didn't really want to play video games today. The deer were out there, and Hunter was eager to go bring one down. But if he didn't accept her challenge, she'd never stop rubbing it in. Kelton Fielding could sometimes be annoying by accident. Yumi was a master at inflicting torment.

"Fine." Hunter mounted his bike and pedaled off out of the school parking lot onto McCall Memorial Trail, the sweet paved bike trail that ran through the woods from way down south of the school along Highway 55, north to the lake, and then northwest when the highway turned. "Race you!"

Yumi laughed. "You're dead, Hunter!"

And he was. Even if she hadn't had a way-better bike, Yumi was still one of the fastest kids in the whole sixth grade. They sped along past boulders and trees as the trail hooked back to Third Street, the main road where Highway 55 cut through town.

Hunter's legs burned as he forced them to put on an extra burst of speed, closing the gap to within three bike lengths as the trail passed the back of Ridley's Grocery Store. She laughed. She actually laughed, before shifting gears and speeding up, passing Tackle Tom's Bait Shop.

The trail turned to the west at the trailhead near the beach just past Hotel McCall. That's where Yumi rolled to a halt and waited for Hunter to catch up.

"Someday I'll beat you." Hunter puffed, looking out over the great expanse of Payette Lake, afternoon sunlight shimmering on the dark water rippling in the gentle breeze. The mountains beyond the lake could get a dusting of snow in the next few weeks. The lake was very low, a ribbon of darker sand along the shore showing how far up the water came in summer.

Hunter always found the beach sad in the fall. The big crowds that would swim or play on the sand in the bright summer were gone. Now only one older woman walked her dog along the shore. The dog squatted and shook a little as he dropped a big turd next to the water.

"You going to stand there all night, waiting to see Sharlie?" Yumi said, already walking her bike over to cross the highway.

Sharlie was the monster that people said lived in the deep part of the lake. When Hunter was a little kid, he absolutely believed the creature was real. After all, his parents and grand-parents all swore she was out there. Now, of course, he knew they were just messing with him. But still, there were some people around town who swore they were certain Sharlie swam the depths or that they'd seen her.

They parked their bikes in the shed behind Wine O'Clock and went into the store. The aroma of so many scented candles always made Hunter feel like he was stepping inside a pie. Yumi complained sometimes that it stank like too much perfume, but her mom always laughed and pointed out that she made a ton of money selling candles.

Aunt Tomoko stood on a three-step ladder. As usual, her wrists jangled with a few charm bracelets, and a couple of glass, ceramic, or wood pendants made by regional artists hung by gold or silver chains from her neck. She sold pendants, charms, and bracelets and things, displaying them on a rack in the corner. She was placing wine signs on a higher shelf. *"Wine Gets Better with Age. I Get Better with Wine." "I Just Want to Drink Wine and Pet My Dog." "Go Ahead and Wine a Little." "Girls Just WINEa Have Fun"* and *"Wine Is the Answer ... What Is the Question?"* All the wine slogans were painted onto little boards and beaten up a little to look old.

"Hey, kiddo!" Aunt Tomoko said from the top of the ladder. "Hi, Hunter! How are you two? How was school?"

Yumi ignored the school question like any normal kid would. "Ugh. Wine signs? Really, Mom? Those things are so dumb. That one literally says, *'You Had Me at Wine.'* What does that even mean?"

Aunt Tomoko glanced around to make sure no customers

were within earshot. "I made these myself! I stenciled all of them by hand on boards I got free when a friend tore down his old barn. Each 'dumb sign' costs me less than two dollars to make, and I sell them for twenty. I sell a ton of them!" She laughed when Yumi shook her head. "You kids hungry? Can I get you cheese and crackers? Some olives?"

"Actually, we were going to the arcade. Hunter was going to try to get his *Ms. Pac-Man* high score back from me," Yumi said.

Aunt Tomoko laughed again. She was an upbeat person like that. Hunter was pretty sure he'd never met anyone nicer. "Yumi, you shouldn't be taking all the high scores. He worked hard at *Ms. Pac-Man* last summer."

Yumi put her hands on her hips. "Then he can work hard to get the score back. I'm not going to sabotage my own game just to spare someone's feelings. All's fair in video games."

Hunter's phone buzzed. A text from his father: *I'll be done soon. You ready?*

Hunter held the phone up, trying to act disappointed. "Wish I could stay and play, but Dad's about ready, so . . ."

"Chicken," Yumi said.

"Well, good luck on your first big hunting trip." Aunt Tomoko grinned. "Tell your father I said hello. Tell him to stop in sometime. Your mother too."

"Sure," Hunter said as he headed for the back door.

"Yumi, your father called," Aunt Tomoko said in a quieter voice as Hunter went outside. He didn't catch the rest of what she said, but he could hear the tension in her voice. Hunter had overheard enough bits of conversation—whispered or murmured in that way parents had when discussing stuff they didn't want their kids to hear—to know Uncle Rick was having serious troubles.

Among other issues, he was pretty much living at the family hunting cabin full-time. Hunter took his bike out of the shed and rode down the block to Dad's law office. He wasn't sure what was happening with Uncle Rick, but he was sure he was ready for his first hunt.

CHAPTER 2

HUNTER'S DAD ALWAYS SAID THAT APPEARANCE MATTERS in the legal profession. People are reluctant to hire a lawyer who works in a shed, and in a trial a jury is less likely to believe a lawyer who's dressed like a bum or looks like he's clueless. So, while some buildings in McCall were made to look rustic, like log-cabin-type structures, Dad's office had a formal red-brick front, and inside had a lot of dark woodwork, bookshelves stuffed with boring thick lawbooks, and fancy-looking furniture and lamps.

Hunter entered the main waiting room, where Mom sat on one of the two small sofas facing the central coffee table, reading a novel. "Mom, what are you doing here?" Hunter asked. "Are you coming with us?"

She looked up at him and smiled. "Oh no. I'm looking forward to a quiet house and two days of uninterrupted reading." She liked stories with characters who worked in libraries or read a lot, and nonfiction about the history or other elements of books. "I'm surprised I beat you here. What took you so long?"

"Was with Yumi," Hunter said. That usually explained it all. "Dad texted me. Is he ready to go?"

Mom tossed back her dark hair and laughed. "I don't know which of you is more excited. Your father was shocked when I showed up here without you. He sent his receptionist home early. He said he'd hurry with a few last-minute work details to close out the week. He doesn't want to waste a minute."

"Neither do I," Hunter said. "Just hope I can hit something, you know?"

"Last time I was at the lodge, your grandpa said your shooting has improved so much you just might inherit his nickname."

Hunter wrinkled his nose. "Sureshot Higgins? No, thanks."

Mom laughed again. "Well, nickname or not, you're a good shooter. You'll do fine."

That wasn't what Hunter had meant. He was glad Mom was here. Sometimes it was easier to talk to Mom rather than Dad about certain things. But before he could explain the true nature of his worries, the smoked-glass door to Dad's office flew open and Hunter's father emerged. "Whew! And that's the workweek."

Dad swept through the waiting area in his usual confident way, leaning down to kiss Mom.

Mom tilted her head a little. "Is that really what you wore today?"

Dad patted his dark jeans and light blue button-up dress

shirt. "Casual Friday! Sport coat's in my office. This way I don't have to change, and we can get going."

Mom slipped her bookmark in her book and stood up. "Well, good luck, you two. Be safe. Wear your blaze-orange vests."

"Well, yeah," said Hunter. "We'll be rifle hunting."

Mom drew him in for a hug. "I know, but I hear a lot of young hunters in my library who don't quite trust that deer are color-blind, and insist on camouflage only."

Dad put his arm around her shoulders. "The Higgins family always wears blaze-orange when hunting with rifles."

"I knew that, I guess. I don't want to be one of those overprotective kind of moms. It's just hard to believe my boy is so grown up." Mom smiled. "Be safe. Good hunting."

THEY WERE SOON IN DAD'S PICKUP AND HEADING OUT OF town on their way to the family hunting cabin.

After driving in silence for a couple of minutes, Dad spoke up. "So you ready for this weekend?"

Hunter was, and he said so, but there was more, only he didn't know the right way to bring it up with his father.

Eventually he asked, "Did you take a deer your first time?"

"I did," Dad said. "Not what you'd call a big trophy buck, but respectable. I had most of it made into jerky to eat out on the hunting trail through the rest of the season. I loved it, out there in nature, just me, my old man, and his dad. Do you remember your Great-Grandpa Higgins?"

"A little," Hunter said. "He'd always pretend to box me when I was little."

Dad laughed. "That's right. He's the one who bought our hunting preserve and put the first tiny wood cabin on it."

"And Grandpa built the lodge?" Hunter asked.

"*We* built the lodge when I was a junior in high school. Grandpa's construction company had scored some great contracts the year before that, resurfacing most of the highway almost clear to Boise. So he built the lodge to keep the family tradition alive. You may think it's just a simple pole barn with a part-finished interior, but it took a *lot* of work."

This was the first Hunter had heard about this. "You know how to do all that stuff?" Hunter asked.

Dad shot him a quick, confused look. "Are you serious? I thought you knew."

Hunter knew Grandpa had built up a big construction and earthmoving business, working on highways, bridges, and big industrial sites, but Dad hadn't talked about working with Grandpa very much.

Dad shrugged. "I worked off and on for my old man starting when I was sixteen. Full-time during summer back in college. So, *yes*, I know how to do all that stuff. Most of it. Well, a lot of it. Hardest part of building the lodge wasn't building it, but getting the cement and the rest of the building materials back there. Your grandfather had to re-bulldoze the road on our land leading to the site first so the trucks wouldn't get stuck. But I helped dig and level the site, pour and finish the concrete slab foundation, get the steel frame set up right. Everything right down to hanging, taping, and finishing the drywall on the rooms inside."

Dad cracked his knuckles, a habit Hunter hated but which his father seemed to get into more the closer he was to hunting or manual labor, and the farther he got from his law office.

Dad turned north onto Warren Wagon Road, heading up the west side of Lake Payette, and suddenly McCall was left behind. They were into the woods. Well, sort of the woods. Cabins and houses were packed in pretty tight, especially on the land between the road and the lake. It had always seemed to Hunter that nobody had planned very well for where the cabins might go. Instead they were all wedged into pure chaos, the front of one opening right next to the back of another, roads to access them zigzagging among all the buildings, some of them large and expensive-looking, some more simple shacks.

"Yeah, your grandpa was disappointed, kind of hurt when I didn't go into the family business. He didn't try to stop me from pursuing a law career, but . . . well, there was some real tension. But that was a long time ago. Hunting brought us back together. For a while, hunting and fishing were about the only connection we had."

"I never knew any of that," Hunter said, impressed by this revelation of his father's broad set of skills and surprised there had been trouble between Dad and Grandpa. Some of his friends at school had divorced parents, but dads and sons couldn't split up, could they? Anyway, aside from the occasional mild argument over politics, the two of them seemed to get along fine now.

"You learn a lot on hunting trips." Dad was watching the road, but somehow the look in his eyes made Hunter think he was staring much farther than the next curve in the highway. He was quiet for a moment. "Yeah, you'll learn a lot."

Hunter wanted to ask what he might learn, but he sensed that now wasn't the right time, and that his Dad wouldn't even be able to tell him, at this moment, exactly what he was supposed to learn. He said nothing as ancient classic rock played softly on the radio.

They continued up Warren Wagon Road. Eventually the highway came out of the deep evergreen woods a little, curving to the right to run closer to the lake. Out across the water loomed the north end of the great peninsula that reached up into the lake. Porcupine Point, and in the distance beyond that, Cougar Island.

"My whole life, minus a few years in college down in Boise, is on this lake. Swimming, boating, and fishing on it in summers. Hunting in the woods around it." Dad sighed. "Fell in love with your mother out on my dad's fishing boat when—"

"She caught a trout twice as big as yours," Hunter said. "I know. I've heard the story."

Dad laughed. "I suppose you have. But, of course, it wasn't just the fish. That was only part of it. What I mean is, our lives are intricately connected to the land. No matter how many roads we build up or how much of our time is spent on computers and phones, we are still connected to this place. Nothing reminds me of that so much as hunting."

Hunter had been twisting his seat belt in his hands and finally blurted out something that had been hovering at the edge of his thoughts for weeks, ever since Dad had told him he could come on this hunting trip. "I'm nervous." Instantly his cheeks felt hot.

Dad frowned. "Nervous about what?"

The heat spread down his neck, and he was sure he was flaring red. "I don't know," he said quietly.

"What is it? You mean about hunting?"

Hunter nodded. "It's just that I . . ." How could he explain this without sounding dumb, or weak and afraid? He was probably too late.

"You've taken the hunting safety course. You've been taught gun safety all your life. You've had plenty of practice shooting. You're a great shooter. What's the problem?"

Hunter forced himself to let go of the seat belt. "What if I can't do it?"

"Are you kidding me? You were dropping most of the targets on the range at the lodge, even way out at three hundred yards. You've got this."

That wasn't what Hunter meant. But he couldn't figure out how to tell Dad what was on his mind. In the Higgins family, turning twelve was a big deal. It meant he was allowed to watch more grown-up TV shows and movies and he could stay up later. Twelve meant he was old enough to go hunting with the men.

They were trusting him to be old enough to be around them when they were having fun, talking about grown-up things, cussing, and having a good time.

If he told Dad, Grandpa, or Uncle Rick that he wasn't sure he wanted to kill an animal, they'd think he was pathetic. Worse, they'd make fun of him, call him a little girl or a crybaby, the way guys do. Once, at lunch in school, Hunter had made the mistake of saying he wasn't very interested in playing football next year in seventh grade. He'd been able to salvage what was left of his reputation by saying he'd been joking and ripping on any hypothetical guy who wasn't interested in laying on a hard hit against an opposing player on the football field.

"You really think I can do this?" Hunter breathed.

"Hunter." Dad sounded like he was shocked his son would even ask the question. "I know you can."

They followed Warren Wagon Road past high stone cliffs on the left and the broad expanse of beach at the north end of the lake. Hunter watched the winding river and marshland out his window. Eventually they passed the right turn for East Side Road that would have taken them on a bumpy drive down the east bank of the lake. They continued north for a long time until turning onto the narrow gravel Deer Lane. Finally they stopped outside the gate to the private road that led to the Higgins hunting lodge.

Dad handed over a silver key and nodded toward the white, slightly rusted cattle gate, a big NO HUNTING—NO TRESPASSING sign hung from the middle. Hunter smiled a little. Maybe it was no big deal, getting out to unlock the gate—the padlock on the chain was new and easy—but the way Dad just assumed he knew what to do, and trusted him to do it as if he were a normal adult, made him feel welcome and a part of all this. He swung the gate open, Dad drove through, and Hunter closed and locked it again.

The gravel driveway snaked its way up the slope and headed farther back into the woods for about half a mile.

"Remember as much of this trip as you can." Dad laughed a little. "I mean, I *named* you Hunter because of how much our family loves this sport."

"It would be easier to remember this if Grandpa would allow me to document it with my phone."

Dad waved the idea away. "You don't need your phone out here. You're on that thing too much anyway. We're all on our phones too much. To really live, especially to live nature, you have to leave the internet and all that gadgetry behind."

"Well, there goes my Snapchat streak," Hunter said. He laughed when Dad shot him the funniest look, an expression of mixed horror, annoyance, and doubt. "I'm kidding!" Then Dad laughed too. Actually, it was good to be here in the last land of no cell service. Hunter enjoyed the break from his friends' collective online buzz.

Dad pulled up onto the wide gravel parking plateau in front of the lodge. From outside, the lodge was plain. A tan aluminum building with a big roll-up garage door, and a door for people next to it. A few windows spaced evenly about every six feet along either side. One of Grandpa's big yellow backhoe tractors was parked over by the straw bales where the targets were already hanging for their archery range. In the near distance behind the clearing the dark rock face of the steep cliff rose a solid hundred feet.

Dad parked the truck and killed the engine. The two of them sat for a long moment, together in the still silence that fell so heavily after the motor vibration of the long drive had finally stopped. "You're twelve now, Hunter," Dad said quietly. "Your childhood is coming to an end. Now you're a young adult, entering an amazing time of discovery. Some people have the greatest time of their lives through their teenage years. Some have it harder than others. But whatever happens, these years will be a big part of making you the person you are to become. So try to enjoy and remember these times, because once they're gone, they're gone, and they don't ever come again."

Without saying anything more, Dad opened his door and climbed out of the truck. Hunter did the same, his shoes crunching on the gravel as he walked around to the back to get his bag and his gun. He closed his eyes and took a deep breath as he headed toward the building. Hunter had been to the lodge before, but this time everything was different and the experience felt completely new. This was really happening. His first hunting trip had begun.

CHAPTER 3

PEOPLE WERE SOMETIMES IMPRESSED WHEN HUNTER talked about his family's hunting lodge. They must have imagined a rich, fancy mountaintop mansion. Hunter always had to explain that the "lodge" was simply what his family called it. Really, it was a big steel and aluminum box, half giant garage and half finished house space.

The garage half had workbenches, tools, and cabinets along both side walls, and two large deep freezers along the back wall away from the big bay door. One of Grandpa's hobbies was woodworking, and he did a lot of projects here. The family also stored the tractor, three snowmobiles, two four-wheelers, a few kayaks, two canoes, and an assortment of bicycles, the combined recreational vehicle fleet of Grandpa, Hunter's Dad, Uncle Rick, Aunt Lorie, and their families.

The back of the garage was mostly a big blank white wall, with half a dozen mounted trout and bass, three deer heads, and some stuffed ducks and mallards standing on little wood platforms. One small room jutted out into the garage in the corner. Inside were white plastic walls, stainless steel counters, and a center table. Saws and other tools hung on the wall. When not in use, it was perfectly clean and kept locked. That's where they cleaned fish or butchered the animals they killed in the hunt.

Hunter looked longingly at the snowmobiles. "I read an article that said it's supposed to snow a lot this winter."

"Hope so," said Dad. "Your uncle Mike was up here last weekend. He says he's laying claim to a few pounds of whatever meat we take on account of how he cleaned and cleared our snowmobile trail all the way out to the county's old railroad trail."

"That's great," Hunter said. Nobody loved snowmobiling more than his aunt Lorie's husband, Uncle Mike. The county snowmobile trail was on the leveled bed of long-torn-away train tracks. A branch line shot off of that for about a hundred yards to a gold mine that had been closed for a hundred years or something. A small creek crossed the branch line about twenty yards before the mine. The rails and ties were gone, and where there had once been a bridge there remained only what snowmobile riders called Stone Cold Gap. The trail angled up sharply just before where the bridge had been, and then there was nothing but a gap of ten feet until the trail resumed on the other side of the stream, the icy creek gurgling twenty feet below. Uncle Mike was the only man Hunter had ever seen even attempt to jump Stone Cold Gap. Just when it looked like he was going to smash too low into the opposite bank, he stuck the landing. "Don't tell your aunt Lorie," was all he'd said about it.

Through the double doors in the back wall of the garage, Hunter and his father passed into the finished living quarters of the lodge.

No matter how many times he saw it, Reagan always surprised Hunter. Reagan was Grandpa's fully stuffed trophy bear, shot in 1984, the third-largest bear ever taken in Idaho. When Hunter was a little kid, it had terrified him with its dark fur, long claws, and sharp teeth exposed in an everlasting silent roar. Now he understood it as an amazing example of Grandpa's hunting prowess.

Nobody who visited the lodge could fail to grasp the importance of the outdoors in general and of hunting in particular to the Higgins family. The place was a museum, a shrine, a temple to hunting. The plain white walls were fast filling with trophies of past hunts. Ten different deer heads and a massive elk trophy were mounted in the open living room/kitchen area, and a bearskin rug decorated the floor space before the TV. At the top of the walls near the ceiling a wallpaper border showed a repeating wilderness landscape with a group of hunters out after beautiful ducks and mallards, noble deer looking on in the distance. The deep greens and browns of the wallpaper border strip circled the entire main room, drawing the place into a camouflaged feel.

Camouflage was a big theme at the lodge. Grandpa's recliner

upholstery boasted one woodland camo pattern. The couch, though old and faded, sported another. If Grandpa had been able to find a camouflage-pattern carpet, he would have had it installed in every room.

The supply of kitchen and bathroom towels was a mixed-up selection of camouflage patterns, images of animals, and scenes with hunters after deer, elk, ducks, and pheasants. The handles on the knives, forks, and spoons in the drawers were fake animal horn. The handles on all drawers and cupboards, even the spindle upon which the toilet paper spun, were made of real deer antler points or cut-off nubs, most of which had been found lying on the ground in the woods after the shed antler season in winter, but some of which had been taken by hunting.

Hunter took it all in with a satisfied smile, his family's hunting lodge, a hunter's paradise, the second home he'd visited hundreds of times, now finally also his base camp for hunting.

"Hey, little man!" Grandpa said, emerging from the kitchen, cracking a can of the cheap beer that the men drank so much at the lodge. "Not so little anymore, though! Are you excited?"

"You bet, Grandpa," Hunter said.

"Your old man help you wash all your hunting clothes?" Grandpa asked. Grandpa and Dad swore it was crucial to take from the deer their advantage of a superior sense of smell by washing all their hunting clothes in special detergent designed to remove all odors—and to shower, the morning before the hunt, using special soap and shampoo designed to do the same to their bodies.

"Sure, Grandpa," Hunter said. "And I brought plenty of Right Guard deodorant." Hunter had started using the stuff last year after his class had been subjected to a video at school about their changing bodies. But he hadn't really brought the scented Right Guard today.

"You better not use that stuff before we go out tomorrow," Grandpa said. "Deer will smell that miles away!"

"But it says *de*odorant right on the can." Hunter was doing a great job holding back his smile.

"It just covers your natural body odor with a perfume scent."

Now Hunter grinned. "Are you telling me my deodorant has been *lying* to me?"

Grandpa burst into laughter. "Hey, you kidder!"

Grandpa gave his son a quick hug. Then his normally happy, confident expression faltered for a tiny moment. "Listen, uh, Rick's been staying in the main bedroom. So why don't you and Hunter set yourselves up in the duck room?"

"He doing any better?" Dad asked quietly.

Grandpa opened his mouth to answer, but glanced at Hunter and stopped himself. He patted Dad on the back. "Everything's fine. Just getting some space. Nothing like coming out to the wilderness to get a man back on track."

Dad nodded and carried their bags and gun cases back to the bedroom decorated with at least eight stuffed ducks.

"Hunter, I've been looking forward to your first hunt for a long time." Grandpa approached one of the deer trophies that seemed to watch over the big dining-area table. He gazed up at it with an admiring smile and turned to Dad. "Remember this one, David?"

Dad had returned and grabbed a beer for himself and a can of soda for Hunter. "Of course! It was my first. October twenty-second, 1994. I was about Hunter's age when I took that respectable four-by-four with my Remington 788." Dad took a drink. "I was climbing out of this little ravine, and as soon as my head popped up, I saw him munching on a shrub. Beautiful creature. He connected perfectly with the wilderness. And I felt . . . I was connected too, like something magical. Simply incredible. It took me about twenty minutes to quietly and slowly climb up onto his level."

"Because we don't take shots if we're not set up and stable," Grandpa said, holding up his beer in a salute to Hunter.

"Another five minutes or so carefully checking the area behind the buck."

"Because we don't take shots that have even a chance of being unsafe," Grandpa said. "Even if it means giving up an easy shot and letting an animal get away."

Hunter nodded. He knew all this. He'd heard it many times.

"Finally, I lined up the shot. That buck fever, that intense adrenaline rush, coursed through me," Dad said. "The deer perked up and seemed to see me an instant before I pulled the trigger. Perfect shot. He bounded away as most deer do when shot. But six steps later, he dropped."

Talking over old hunts was a key part of the family's time at the lodge. They all knew the story behind every trophy on

the walls and countless more photographs. Hunter would
have thought they would need little plaques under each trophy
as a reminder of when, where, and how it was taken, but for
Grandpa, Dad, and Uncle Rick, it was like time travel. When
they started telling the tale of how they took an animal, they
seemed to transport back to the moment, recalling every little
detail with perfect clarity. Would it be that way for Hunter
someday? He wasn't so sure.

Hunter watched his father eyeing that deer's head, a look of
admiration on his face. He had talked about how the buck was
beautiful. Magical. Dad had felt connected to him. How could
he kill something to which he felt connected?

Dad and Grandpa took seats on stools around the island
countertop in the kitchen, like they usually did, catching up with
each other about work, and reminiscing about great times they'd
had hunting in the past.

Hunter perched on a stool at the far end of the counter,
eager to be part of these kinds of fond stories, a part of the family
memories.

"Chili should be warmed up in a little bit," Grandpa said.
"I know you like venison chili."

"Oh yeah," Hunter said. He loved the stuff. He loved venison
and deer jerky, as well as duck, and wild turkey on Thanksgiving.
He wasn't one of those people, hippies, Grandpa called them,
who thought hunting was a violation of an animal's rights.
Animals weren't people.

But they were alive. Hunter hoped he could kill when the

moment came. He wanted to. He *would* kill if—when the time came. He was a Higgins. His freaking name was *Hunter*! He was born to hunt. He stared at his Dad's majestic first deer. Hunter would kill when the time came. He would. He absolutely would.

After about an hour of Dad telling Grandpa about a complicated situation that came up after a wealthy client died and his kids began fighting over the inheritance, and Grandpa telling Dad about a new highway resurfacing contract he was planning to bid on, Grandpa turned his laptop around and showed a short black-and-white video clip of a buck, a solid four-by-four, strutting through, looking almost right at the camera. "Pretty good one."

"Where was this?" Dad asked.

"Near that scrape down by the creek, by the north crossing," Grandpa said.

Grandpa had four motion-activated trail cameras that he'd set up at different places around the property, wherever bucks were making rubs on trees or scrapes in the dirt, part of their bizarre way of impressing does. To save battery life, the cameras only recorded thirty-second videos.

"He'll be great to take in a few years." Grandpa turned the computer back around and continued clicking through the hundreds of videos he'd collected on the four different memory cards. The man loved this almost as much as hunting. He looked through trail cam footage for hours every time they came to the lodge.

From outside came the low rumble of an engine, the crunch of tires on gravel.

Grandpa looked up from his deer footage. "Ah, Rick's back."

Hunter hopped off his stool and ran for the door. "I'll see if he needs help carrying anything."

Uncle Rick was one of the coolest guys Hunter knew. He had been a fire jumper, parachuting into the wilderness to fight forest fires. That meant he was tough, could carry heavy gear, and could get himself out of dangerous situations. He'd been in the Army National Guard too, stationed in what he had called a rough province of Afghanistan. Hunter had never heard many details about what had happened to Uncle Rick over there, but he'd picked up enough clues to know his uncle was kind of an action hero. He'd taken out some terrorists and saved his men, winning the Bronze Star Medal.

Hunter met him in the garage. "Hey, Uncle Rick. What's the sitrep?" It was the greeting the two of them had always shared. "Sitrep" was military talk meaning "situation report." It sounded way more cool than "what's up."

"Nephew!" Uncle Rick said with a big grin. "Just getting geared up for a big hunt. I don't even know the last time the Higgins family had *two* young ones out for their first hunts."

Hunter frowned. "Two?"

Yumi came into the garage folding her arms. "More like three."

"Three?" Hunter asked. What was going on here?

Another girl walked in. Hunter rubbed his eyes. The garage was rather dark, and the bright light from outside silhouetted whoever was standing in the doorway. She turned her head a little and a breeze caught her curly hair. The light flashed on her glasses. "Hey, Hunter," she said.

He wasn't dreaming. It wasn't a hallucination. Somehow, Annette Willard had just walked into the lodge.

Hunter felt his cheeks grow hot, melting away the comfort he usually felt here on his family's land. Suddenly he wasn't quite sure how to stand, and he shifted his weight. Grandpa had often talked about how one could never know what to expect when hunting. Whatever Hunter had thought was going to happen, he absolutely hadn't predicted Yumi and Annette to suddenly arrive.

"Surprise." Annette smiled. "Yumi and I are going hunting with you."

CHAPTER 4

WHAT WAS YUMI EVEN DOING HERE? SHE WAS GREAT, yeah, Hunter's cousin and one of his best friends. But in the Higgins family, for generations, hunting was mostly a guys' thing—a men's thing. Granted, Hunter had never heard anyone talk about rules against girls hunting with them, but part of the reason he was looking forward to this weekend so much was his chance to be one of the guys. It was like one of those coming-of-age ceremonies he had read about in his social studies book.

Anyway, for some reason Yumi didn't even seem to want to be here. Annette looked more excited than her.

Annette Willard! Now that she was here, everything was thrown off. Hunter would have to act all . . . he didn't even know. The point was he'd have to act differently. What was Yumi doing?

Whatever she was doing, Yumi couldn't resist smiling when Grandpa picked her up and swung her around in a big hug.

"Grandpa, come on!" She laughed a little. "I'm too old for this."

He put her down. "Nonsense. You're too old when my back says you're too old."

"Yeah, because what I really want to do is hurt your back and ruin your whole weekend," Yumi said.

Grandpa waved away her concern. "Bah. I'm fine. I'll always be fine." He turned to Annette. "And who might you be? Yumi's great friend, I take it?"

"Annette Willard," Annette said. "Pleased to meet you, sir."

"Sir?" Grandpa put his hand over his chest, joking like he was shocked she'd used the word. "I have eighty men and four women working for me, and I don't let any of them call me 'sir.'" He offered a handshake. "Call me James."

Annette actually shook his hand, with a full firm grip, like an adult. "Nice to meet you, James."

Hunter watched this all in wonder. Who shook hands? Nobody his age.

"One rule while you're a guest here at the Higgins lodge, Ann," Grandpa said. "There are no guests. While you're here, the place is yours. Do not be shy. Now, you coming hunting with us?"

"I'd love to," Annette said.

"Have you fired a gun before? Have you taken the state's hunter safety course? Do you have a license?"

"A BB gun. No. And no," said Annette. She pulled a small blue spiral notebook from her back pocket. Hunter had seen her writing in it many times. "But I have a notebook. And I'd love to write about this hunting trip for the McCall Middle School newspaper."

Grandpa's regular jokey tone turned serious. Not angry, but serious. "I'm glad you're here, and of course you should come along and write all about our adventure. But since you haven't passed the hunter course and you're not familiar with firearms, you will not touch any of the guns we have around here. At all. And when we go out, you'll need to follow all the directions from me, and my sons David and Rick. The absolute most important rule is safety. If you're being unsafe I'll have Rick take you home."

Instead of being intimidated Annette only nodded, as she quickly wrote in her notebook. "Under-stood . . . com-pletely," she enunciated as she concentrated on writing.

Annette looked up and took in the room, her gaze focusing upon Reagan. "Wow! Is that a real bear? Did you shoot it yourself? I'd love to hear that story."

"It is a real bear." Grandpa brightened. There was no story he loved as much as the tale of when he shot Reagan. "Well, a real taxidermied bear. Yes, I shot it. Back in '84, he was the third-largest bear ever taken in the state. I call him Reagan."

"Reagan?" Annette asked. "Like the president?"

"Yep," said Grandpa. "Ronald Reagan was running for reelection back in 1984. And he had this fantastic campaign ad."

"Oh no," Yumi said. "Here it comes."

Hunter laughed.

Uncle Rick held his hands up with fingers curled like claws. He spoke in a deep voice. "There is a bear in the woods."

Hunter closed his eyes and tried to remember the words of the ad.

Dad recited the next line. "For some people, the bear is easy to see."

"Others don't see it at all!" Hunter blurted out.

Annette looked from one person to another, writing fast to take notes.

"Some people say the bear is tame," Grandpa continued. "Others say it's vicious and dangerous."

"Since no one can really be sure who is right . . ." Dad said.

". . . isn't it smart to be as strong as the bear?" Uncle Rick said.

"If there is a bear!" Hunter joined the men in finishing the old commercial.

It was a silly tradition.

Annette clapped. "Bravo! How can you possibly remember a political ad from so long ago?"

Hunter wanted to know how Annette could be so comfortable, not shy at all, around adults like this. Hunter was part of the family and still didn't feel so open with them. Annette somehow talked to them as if they were all old friends.

Grandpa seemed impressed with her as well. He let go his big booming laugh. "Reagan's landslide victory over Walter Mondale in the 1984 election was exciting. That commercial was on TV all the time back in those days, and since I killed the bear back then, everybody kept saying, 'There's a bear in the woods . . .' and eventually I just kind of memorized the rest."

"OK if we go out to shoot?" Yumi asked.

The men all exchanged a look. "Sure," Grandpa said. "If it's OK with your dads."

"Weapons safety. Range safety at all times," said Uncle Rick.

"Oh cool!" said Annette. "What are the rules?"

"Muzzle awareness," Uncle Rick explained. "Keep your rifle pointed downrange at all times. Load and chamber only when you're in position ready to fire, not before. Clear the rifle and put the weapon on safe when you're done firing. Nobody goes downrange until all weapons are cleared and on safe."

"Never assume a weapon is clear unless you've checked it yourself," Yumi said. "I know."

A few minutes later, Yumi, Annette, and Hunter were out on the shooting range behind the lodge. Hunter carried the Remington 783 rifle. Yumi had a box of 6.5 Creedmoor shells, three sets of earplugs, and three four-round magazines.

One thing handy about having a grandfather in the construction and earthmoving business was that it was no problem for him to get a bulldozer to push up a high dirt berm to stop rounds at the back of the range. Without that, all that was back there was the stone cliff, rising high above them. Rock was a terrible material behind a shooting range. It presented a serious ricochet danger.

"Wow," Annette said. "So this is where you practice shooting guns?" She pointed at the series of plastic, loosely deer-shaped targets at various positions and distances back along the range. "And they just let you bring a gun and real bullets out here all by yourselves?"

Yumi shrugged. "Yeah. I guess when you grow up around guns like us, they stop being so scary or mysterious. Me and Hunter have been shooting for two years."

"Really?" Annette sounded truly impressed. "Are you good at it?"

"I'm OK. But Hunter's really the best," Yumi said evenly.

Hunter's cheeks flared red, and he busied himself working with the bolt action, again to re-check and make sure the chamber was empty. He pretended to examine something near the trigger.

Annette held her hand up like a sun visor. "Can you even shoot the ones far in the back?"

They'd reached the old picnic table by the firing point. Hunter busied himself scuffing his boot in the dirt to draw the safety line. It helped make clear what area counted as downrange, and how far back observers had to stay. Plus it gave Hunter something to do even as he answered Annette quietly, "Sometimes."

Yumi looked questioningly from Annette to Hunter and back again. Then she laughed. "Sometimes? More like most of the time. Basically all the time. Hunter is a great shot. Grandpa says he's going to turn over to Hunter his old nickname 'Sureshot Higgins.'"

Why was Yumi saying all that? Even if it was kind of true. She was acting like he was all great?

"Hey, let's shoot before we lose the light," Hunter said.

"I know I'm not allowed to handle the guns," Annette said,

"but can you show me how all this works?" She pulled out her ever-present blue notebook. "I'll take notes."

This was crazy. Not only had Yumi crashed what was kind of supposed to be *his* weekend, but he was supposed to concentrate on shooting and on hunting . . . with Annette here? It was too much.

Yumi set her things down on the picnic table, put in earplugs, and handed hearing protection to Hunter and Annette. She took the rifle from Hunter, keeping it pointed downrange at the ground, lifting the round black ball at the end of the little bolt handle and pulling the bolt back to check that the chamber was empty. "This is a Remington 783 bolt-action rifle." Yumi spoke loudly to be heard while everyone had earplugs in. "It is chambered to fire a six-point-five Creedmoor round and operates with a four-round magazine."

Yumi showed the safety switch to Annette. "So, loading it. Keep the safety on. Make sure the bolt is forward by keeping the handle forward and turned down. Then take a loaded magazine, slap it into the bottom of the rifle here." She smiled. "If the bullets in the mag aren't pointing forward, you're doing it wrong." She slid in the magazine. "Keep the gun pointed downrange." She demonstrated as she described the process for Annette. "Turn the bolt handle up, pull it all the way back, then push it back forward and lock the handle back down. Now the round is chambered. When I turn off the safety, the rifle will fire when I pull the trigger."

Yumi lowered herself down on her belly, her finger straight and not curled over the trigger. Her left elbow was pressed to the ground and her hand up as support under the barrel.

Hunter watched his cousin. Whatever she had said about his shooting wasn't an indication that she couldn't shoot. She fired and knocked down the target at a hundred and fifty yards. She quickly flipped the bolt handle up, pulled it back to eject the spent bullet casing, pushed the bolt forward again, and swung it back down. In about two seconds she was ready to fire again, and she dropped the two-hundred-yard target.

Yumi continued shooting like that, switching out magazines, until she'd fired twelve rounds, dropping nine out of twelve targets. She'd missed both three-hundred-yard targets, and she must have pulled the trigger too hard on one shot because she missed an easy one-hundred-yarder.

Hunter reloaded the magazines as the girls tipped the targets back up. When the girls were safely back behind the line, he settled into the prone position to take his turn. The smooth wood of the rifle felt good in his hands, familiar and natural. He worked the bolt action to chamber a round and turned off the safety. He aimed at one of the two farthest targets. Remembering to relax and control his breathing, Hunter breathed in, out, in, and fired. The target dropped. He was dimly aware of Annette clapping behind him. But mostly Hunter zeroed in, joining with the rifle, as though it were a part of him and he were a part of it.

A non-shooter would probably never be able to understand what this felt like. Hunter didn't consciously remember shooting fundamentals like breath control and a smooth, easy trigger pull. Those skills were simply a part of him, and he felt powerful, unstoppable as the targets fell. The other three-hundred-yarder dropped. Then both two-fifties in quick succession. Everything else faded away as he fired, until the last of his twelve rounds was spent and the echo of his final shot rolled out over the range with all twelve targets down, the sharp burned-pepper smell of gunpowder connecting him now with memories of all the practice that had been required to achieve this kind of success with a rifle.

"What did I tell you?" Yumi said after they'd all removed their earplugs. "Hunter 'Sureshot' Higgins."

Hunter stayed on the ground a moment longer. Fine. He could shoot. Even with the distraction of Annette being around. But targets were one thing. Deer were another. He could shoot. But could he kill?

He slapped the ground in frustration. Why did Yumi have to come? Why on earth did she have to bring Annette? If Hunter messed up tomorrow, it would be a million times worse with them around.

CHAPTER 5

"LOOK AT THESE SNOWMOBILES AND FOUR-WHEELERS AND things. There's so much," Annette said, surveying what Grandpa sometimes called the "big toys" back in the garage part of the lodge.

"Yeah." Hunter shrugged. "Well, it all belongs to the whole family."

"You all must have so much fun here."

Hunter smiled. It was neat how Annette allowed herself to be excited about things, instead of holding back, acting like everything was no big deal, the way the cool kids always did.

Annette turned back to Yumi and Hunter. She smiled too. "I would never want to leave this place."

"Yeah, well, some of us *don't* leave here," Yumi said quietly.

As Yumi and Annette put the rifle and extra ammo into the gun locker, Hunter headed into the warmth of the living quarters.

"I don't know, Dad!" Uncle Rick spoke sharply. "OK? I don't

know! It's been ten years, but I can't . . . I mean, the dreams have come on sharp lately, and—" Uncle Rick broke off, his voice tightening up like he was about to cry.

Hunter stood behind Reagan. So far nobody had seen him or heard him come in.

"Hey," Dad said. "It's OK. From what I've read, lots of soldiers and veterans have these problems. It's good to hear you're talking to someone—"

"All the shrinks at the VA want to do is medicate me. Get me on this or that drug," said Uncle Rick. "Well, I won't do it."

"Son—"

"And I can't be around Yumi and Tomoko if I'm all messed up," said Uncle Rick. "I just need more time. What's wrong with that?"

Dad answered. "Well, how much longer—"

"It doesn't matter," Grandpa said, cutting Dad off quickly. "It doesn't matter! Rick, you stay out here as long as you need to. Get yourself right. It's fine. That's final."

The door to the garage opened and the girls came back in. Hunter emerged from behind Reagan, quickly joining them so the men wouldn't realize he'd been listening.

"Hey!" Uncle Rick said, a little too loudly, a little too cheerfully. "They're back! How was the shooting?"

Any smile or good cheer that Yumi had managed while out on the firing range dropped as fast as any of the targets she'd hit. "Fine," she answered curtly.

"Better than fine," Annette said. "It was amazing. They are both really good at it. Hunter hit them all."

"That's great," said Uncle Rick. "Did you have fun shooting, Yumi?"

"Sure. Whatever," she said. "Chili ready?"

Uncle Rick stood there silently, gripping the island countertop.

Hunter watched them both. He exchanged a look with Annette, but the connection made his cheeks flare hot.

"Sure," Grandpa said. "Food's ready. Venison chili. Plus we have cheese and crackers."

Dad went over to the TV and started flipping through the stack of old DVDs. "I know just the thing to get us all in the right spirit."

Yumi sighed. "Oh no. Not *Big Time Bucks*. We've seen all of these a thousand times."

"What's *Big Time Bucks*?" Annette asked.

"It's this boring old—"

"It's great!" Hunter burst out. "It's just hours of hunters taking trophy deer or bighorn sheep. We watch them all the time. It's tradition."

"Sounds great." Annette shot a nervous glance at Yumi, but Yumi just dug into her bowl of chili.

Dad nodded with a big goofy smile and slipped the disc into the player.

Big Time Bucks 16 came on screen. Hunter smiled as he ate his chili, a melted string of the shredded cheese he'd sprinkled on top falling down on his chin. Annette laughed. Hunter quickly wiped his mouth.

Big Time Bucks always kicked off with a hard and fast electric guitar edge and a thumping base with clip after clip of big-time pro hunters taking down magnificent animals, before getting to the first of several live hunts that would be shown on the disc. The camera followed two men clad head-to-toe in camouflage, rolling through a grassy field on a John Deere Gator. They stopped and the film cut to a close-up with the name *Timmy Ballings: Pro Hunter* at the bottom of the screen.

"*Welcome to MegaHunt Adventure Gear's* Big Time Bucks 16," Timmy said as he dismounted from the vehicle and, compound bow in hand, started walking across a grassy field toward a row of trees along a fence line. "*We're out here in northeast Iowa on a fabulous fall day, hoping to take a serious big time buck.*" He lowered his voice to a loud whisper. "*With all this corn for these hungry deer to eat, Iowa has some of the best whitetail deer hunting in the country. These kinds of woods along the field edge are just the perfect place to line up a shot on, maybe a sixteen-, maybe a twenty-point buck. We'll settle in to my tree stand and see what kind of bucks pass our way. Wow! I'm excited!*"

"Why is he breathing so heavy?" Annette asked.

Dad and Uncle Rick laughed.

"You haven't seen anything yet," Yumi said. "This guy is weird. He goes crazy in these videos."

"Hunting is pretty fun," Grandpa said. "It can be exciting. The thrill of the hunt, when you're closing in on a great buck. The adrenaline can really be pumping."

"They call that buck fever," Hunter said. He could hardly wait to experience it himself.

"Right," Yumi said. "If there is buck fever, this guy always catches buck whooping cough." The men laughed, and Yumi smiled a little. It was the first time so far this weekend that Yumi and Uncle Rick had both smiled at the same time. Hunter thought it was a good sign. "Or buck bubonic plague. He's just ridiculous. Plus, he's a grown man and he goes by the name Timmy? He's the mayor of Patheticville."

"Yeah," Uncle Rick said. "I can't stand this guy. He's like a big baby, a disgrace to hunters."

"What do you mean?" Annette said. "He looks pretty tough with that bow and arrow."

"He's not tough!" Yumi said. "He's a freak. You'll see. Let him do his thing. Spoiler alert, almost every hunt on these videos ends in success."

"Which is very different from real life," Grandpa said. "If you're hunting mature bucks, it's not uncommon to go three to five years without shooting a deer."

Timmy Ballings kept whisper-narrating to the camera. "It's a warmish day in late October, but as the sun's lowering in the west, so is the temperature. That's why I'm glad I have MegaHunt Adventure Gear's Fast-Action Hand Warmers in my gloves, and MegaHunt Adventure Gear's Fire-Foot Boot Inserts."

"Does this guy hunt, or is he just a commercial?" Annette asked.

Hunter had watched hundreds of hours of these hunting videos during his visits to the lodge, but he'd mostly focused on the hunting action. Now that he thought about it, the video did seem kind of like a commercial. Annette was right. But a part of him wished she'd be quiet about it. She felt too much like an outsider come in to bash on their family traditions. She wasn't even supposed to be here.

"Well, all these pro hunters are sponsored by different companies who make hunting gear or weapons, so they have some promotional consideration," Dad said.

"*I can hear a lot of activity out in the field, cornstalks rustling,*" Timmy Ballings whispered with a big smile on his face. "*And I saw a little four-point buck come out of the field a while ago. But you don't always want to take the first buck you see, especially a smaller one like that. Oh boy. So, I'm holding out for a bigger—Oh!*" He held his fist over his mouth as if to keep from bursting out. The camera cut to a large twelve-point buck.

"Is he going to be OK?" Annette asked. "He looks like he's going to cry."

"Yep, that's Timmy Ballings," Dad said. "Every time."

"*Oh-ho-ho-oooh!*" Timmy Ballings hissed, slowly bringing his bow up and nocking an arrow. "*I can't . . . I can't believe it! This . . . this is the big time!*"

On-screen, Timmy Ballings slowly raised the bow, using a release to draw back the bowstring. Everybody in the room got quiet for a moment, almost as if making any noise would somehow scare away the deer on the video.

Ballings loosed the arrow. A second later the buck jerked, tried to run, stumbled. Hunter could see its blood, see the surprise and anguish in its wide eyes. The buck tried to take two more steps but then fell, gasping on the ground for just a moment before going still.

Hunter watched the animal's last struggles. This was what hunting, his family's main hobby, was all about. Timmy Ballings could have scored a cleaner kill, dropping the animal faster, but Hunter had heard enough family hunting stories to know perfectly clean kills didn't always happen. He didn't feel sorry for that deer. He didn't.

The video cut to Timmy Ballings inspecting his kill. He was no longer whispering, but kind of gasping, whining, almost sobbing. Tears were in his eyes. "*. . . so beautiful. Suh-huh-huh-ho-ho! Whoa! I saw him coming out of the corn. And I thought . . . I just thought. It's the big time, you know?*"

"This guy is pathetic!" Yumi called out. "He's crying like a baby just 'cause he shot a deer!"

Well, at least he took his shot, Hunter thought. *I might be too much of a baby even to do that.*

AFTER DINNER EVERYONE PLAYED A COUPLE OF ROUNDS OF Uno before they started shutting everything down for the night.

"It's kind of early," Annette said quietly to Yumi and Hunter. "Is everyone really going to bed already?"

"We go out right before dawn," Hunter told Annette.

"During the day, deer find places to hide and bed down. It's tough to find them then. So we go out early, when it's bright enough to see to safely hunt while the deer are still running around trying to find food. Then we return to the lodge and hang out all day. And we go out again just before it starts to get dark at sunset, when the deer are coming back out."

"Which means everybody will be up at zero-dark-thirty," Uncle Rick said. "So, time to hit the rack."

The girls set up sleeping bags on the living room floor. "Well, if there's any trouble," Annette said, "we have Reagan the giant bear here to protect us."

Minutes later Dad and Hunter were settled under the blankets in the two twin beds in the duck room, lights out and the lodge going quiet, save for the sound of coyotes howling in the distant dark woods.

"Big day tomorrow," Dad said sleepily. "This is going to be great."

And Hunter was sure it would be. If only they found the right buck. If only Hunter was in the right position and could manage to shoot straight under pressure. If only he had the nerve to shoot—to kill the animal. If only he didn't make a fool of himself in front of Yumi and, worse, in front of Annette. If only. If only. A lot of hopes rode on "if only." And a lot of fear.

CHAPTER 6

THE BED WAS COMFORTABLE. THE MATTRESS WAS JUST right, not too hard or too soft, not too hot or too cold. He was living the story of the three bears, or in the house of one dead stuffed bear anyway. Hunter relaxed in perfect warmth, wrapped in flannel sheets beneath a checkered quilt his great-grandmother had made long ago out of old hunting clothes of various camouflage patterns. The night should have passed in deep sleep and happy hunting dreams.

But Hunter could hardly sleep. He might have drifted off for a few hours around midnight, but he could not still his heart or his eager imagination enough to settle into a full, deep sleep for long. For at least two hours before wake-up time he lay awake in the bed, imagining the rifle in his hand, stalking quietly through the woods, with his family, with Uncle Rick. Like a soldier. He'd hiked his family's land for years, seen all manner of wildlife. Mule deer, elk, moose, coyotes, raccoons, porcupines, all sorts of snakes, hawks, owls, eagles. He'd even seen a few bears. McCall rested in a valley on a lake wedged right up amid some of the largest national forest areas left in America—a wilderness paradise.

He remembered hiking with Yumi down to what the family called Split Rock Falls, a place where a creek spilled down between two great columns of rock, as though a giant had cleaved the hillside with a colossal ax to let the water flow out. From atop the little cliff, they'd spotted the largest buck either of them had ever seen. For the last two years, he and Yumi had argued about how big he was. Hunter thought he'd counted it a ten-by-ten, but Yumi insisted he was at least a twelve-by-twelve. Either way, he was massive. He had to be a state record buck. He would have provided at least a hundred pounds of meat. As the night wore on, as he waited for morning, Hunter wondered if that buck was still out there. Grandpa had doubted the deer was real, calling him the Phantom. What would it feel like to take a prize so big?

A buck that big, so beautiful, that had survived so many hunting seasons—it seemed a shame to take him down now.

"No," Hunter whispered to himself. He couldn't start thinking that way again. First, that whole idea was backward. It was far worse to shoot the younger bucks that had never had a chance to really live and mate. Better to let them grow. Second, he had to stop being a baby and finally man up about all this. Hunting was great. Hunting required killing. That was the end of it.

The way of the wild was that some animals kill other animals to survive. Either he took his meat from an animal he killed on the hunt, or he went to the store and bought meat killed by someone else. And, like Grandpa often said, hunters were often more kind to the animals they took. Deer, elk, goose, or other game animals lived in the wild until a hunter took the cleanest, quickest kill shot he could make. Meat in the store came from animals that often lived crammed into filthy confinements, injected with hormones and other chemicals, until they were led in terror to the slaughterhouse. The hunting way was better. That was his way. It was.

Finally Dad's phone started playing the quiet spacey music that served as his alarm. That was Hunter's cue. He threw back his covers and rolled from the bed, flicking on a flashlight to see his way to his duffel bag packed with carefully unscented clothes. He'd showered the night before so he could get suited up right away. Pajamas off, long underwear tops and bottoms on. Then he hurried into his jeans. Hunter wasn't wasting a moment of the day.

Dad still hadn't silenced his phone. "Ugh, how could such beautiful music sound so bad?" Dad said quietly, tapping the phone to stop it. He sat up in bed and ran his hand down over his face, scratching his stubbly chin, then seemed to notice Hunter. He chuckled. "Wow! Up and at 'em already. You ready for this?"

Hunter took a deep breath and smiled. "I've been waiting years for this."

Dad moved much slower getting dressed. "Well, you'll have to wait a bit longer. We gotta be out there before dawn. Sure. But even so, nothing happens here before coffee."

Out in the kitchen a while later, everybody was up and ready, showered in no-scent shampoo and dressed warmly in their first de-scented layers, their scentless camouflage coveralls and boots waiting in the garage.

"There's toast. Some Pop-Tarts." Grandpa tapped the brew button on the coffeepot. "Some Cheetos. Or nuke some of last night's chili. Heck, I don't know. Nobody's in diapers here. Get what you want." He sat at the island counter with his favorite *"How 'Bout a Nice Cup of Shut the @#$% Up!"* mug and watched the coffee maker brew.

"Is this the same man?" Annette said very quietly to Yumi.

Yumi shook her head and drew her finger across her neck in the universal kill-it gesture. "Not before coffee," she whispered.

They all ate what they wanted in silence. Hunter enjoyed more chili and was surprised when nobody said he was too young for coffee.

"You eat too much of that chili, you'll have to make an emergency stop in the woods. Better bring some toilet paper," Uncle Rick said. Hunter laughed. Uncle Rick continued, "I'm serious."

Now the girls laughed, and Hunter's cheeks flared red and hot.

Grandpa brightened up by his second cup of coffee. "All right. For those of you new to this, I'll tell ya how it's all going to work. In a minute we'll finish suiting up and then head out in teams. Now, I'll go with Hunter and his dad. Yumi, you'll go with Annette and your dad."

"I want to go with you and Uncle Dave," Yumi said quickly. Uncle Rick looked away. Yumi stood up off her stool and folded her arms. "Please."

Grandpa coughed. "Well, Yumi, I think your dad wanted—"

"No, it's just that I never get to see you, Grandpa. I want to be in your team."

Hunter gripped his mug so tightly that he had to consciously force himself to relax for fear of breaking it.

Grandpa tried again. "But you see, Yumi, part of the point of this weekend is for you and—"

"Right, but it would be so great to go on the hunting team with my grandpa. Plus Annette's kind of profiling you for the middle school newspaper, and—"

"Kind of writing about all of this—" Annette tried.

"But more about you, Grandpa, and—"

"It's fine!" Uncle Rick snapped. "The girls will go with you and David, Dad."

Hunter's dad spoke up. "Then that's four on our team and only two on yours."

Yumi and Annette exchanged a look. Then Yumi glanced at Hunter. He so hoped she wasn't about to say what he thought she was about to say.

"Annette can go on Hunter's team."

She'd said it.

"That's great!" Uncle Rick said quickly. "Three and three. Your team is pushing?"

"Rick—" Grandpa tried.

"We're wasting time," said Uncle Rick. "Your team pushing? Where from? Near Split Rock Falls?"

"They have been eating the clover we planted near there, and they're down there drinking a lot around dawn," Dad offered.

"So you three push them toward the pass on the South Ridge. You know, where we had that little fire a few years ago?" Uncle Rick said.

The South Ridge was a higher rock formation that made a sort of bowl near the edge of their property. Beyond the ridge the land descended on a long slope to the fence marking off public land. And in the middle of the half-bowl ridge was a valley, a gap through which the deer would most likely run if Grandpa's team found deer and scared, or pushed, them toward that ridge. When the deer came through, hopefully Hunter or Uncle Rick would be able to take a shot.

"Let's go!" Uncle Rick went out to the garage. Hunter and Annette looked at each other, and then Hunter put his coffee cup down and headed out.

Uncle Rick said nothing, but stepped into his full-body camouflage jumpsuit. His every movement was angry, sharp, like he was stabbing his legs down through the pants. Then he hurried with the zipper up the front of the outfit, getting it stuck over his chest. He mumbled a curse and fought to fix it.

Hunter and Annette tried to act like they hadn't noticed the tension and continued suiting up. Hunter wore newish boots he'd received last Christmas, and he struggled just a little to push them through the legs of his camo suspender-supported overalls. When he poked his head through the top of his dark green sweatshirt, Uncle Rick was still struggling to unstick the zipper on his coat.

Hunter wished desperately that he could somehow cheer up his favorite uncle. But how? Like his uncle, he felt the anger course through him. It wasn't supposed to go this way. His first hunting trip was supposed to be fun. A celebration. Instead, whatever was going on between Yumi and her dad was threatening to ruin that.

Hunter watched Annette slipping on the smallest of the family's extra hunting gear. Annette was smart, but in a cool and not annoyingly show-offy kind of way. It was great that she was so brave and could talk to anyone without the least shyness. Even if she didn't always have the nicest clothes—the right kind of jeans or whatever—she still looked great. Her reddish brown hair was often in a neat ponytail or curled real nice or in some neat twist that girls somehow understand how to do. And he liked the way her freckled nose wrinkled when she smiled and the way her dark-rimmed glasses sometimes glinted under the classroom's fluorescent lights.

"What?" she said to him with a smile as she slipped on a stocking hat.

"Nothing." Hunter quickly focused his attention on retying his boots for no reason.

Annette was really neat. But Hunter didn't like her or anything. He did not. And he wished more than anything she and Yumi hadn't come here this weekend.

They were all dressed now, Uncle Rick's zipper crisis resolved. He flopped back onto an old couch, drew in a shaky breath, and let it out slowly, his eyes closed. Then again. "We need to move kind of quickly. We might get lucky and spot the deer right away."

Hunter slung his Remington 783, extra magazines loaded with shells in the right cargo pocket on his thigh. Uncle Rick led the way out of the lodge, carrying his McMillan TAC-338, a bolt-action weapon chambered in .338 Lapua Magnum with a five-round magazine. That was a $6,000 rifle, a present Grandpa and Dad bought Uncle Rick when he returned home from the war in Afghanistan.

They stepped out into the cold and dark, emerging into morning early enough to still be called night. On a moonless morning like this, the deep Idaho wilderness transformed into another world. A world full of different sounds, different smells, some kind of strange different energy, and a billion billion stars, like a spray of sparkling ice shining in the cold dark. It was the cold that struck Hunter first, pushing away the last gentle tendrils of sleep, sharpening, hardening him.

"Oh, it's beautiful," Annette whispered.

Hunter wondered if she whispered out of the instinctive understanding that the hunt required quiet, or out of reverence and awe at the beauty all around them.

Probably admiring the beauty, Hunter thought as she pulled out a little penlight and started writing in her blue notebook.

"Hey, Annette," Hunter whispered. "You know, we want to keep the noise and light down. It'll scare away the deer."

"Right," she hissed. "Of course. Sorry."

The three of them started across the gravel parking lot toward the rough trail that would take them in the direction they wanted to go. They'd suffered a bit of a rough start, but it was finally happening. The hunt had begun. Anything could happen now.

CHAPTER 7

UNCLE RICK LED THE WAY, SLOWLY, QUIETLY, THROUGH the dark woods. The other group would depart on a different trail after a few minutes. Hunter had stumbled a little twice, and he tried to focus on the way ahead, on sensing, on joining with the world around him. But he was distracted when Annette kept grabbing the back of his coat for support as they went along. He felt another tug as she slipped again.

Uncle Rick stopped and whispered. "It will begin to brighten a little soon. Relax and let your eyes adjust. It won't take much for us to be able to see enough to find our way."

Hunter smiled. How was Uncle Rick so confident out here? It must be due to his time in the war. Compared to moving around to fight in the deserts of Afghanistan, it must be simple to navigate the woods of Idaho, even if it was dark.

Uncle Rick gently brought Hunter up beside him. "You've shot targets on the range a lot," he said quietly. "You're a good shooter. But today we're not on the range. Our targets aren't plastic." There were long pauses between each of his sentences.

"Today we aim to shoot the living. We're going out to kill. Hunters and other gun owners call guns a tool. A hammer is a tool. A screwdriver. Weapons like we have are nothing short of the power to kill. And that is a sacred power. A holy thing."

"Oh, I wish I could write all this down," Annette said. "Is this very much like war?" Hunter winced at her blatant question. Maybe she thought the better of it too, because she continued quickly, "I mean, if that's an uncomfortable question, you know—"

"I've thought about that a lot," Uncle Rick whispered. "Both here . . . and over there." Hunter wasn't sure his uncle was going to go on, the silence was so long. "And I think the main difference is the power to kill in a hunt is natural, a part of the process of life. The power to kill in war is . . . unnatural. Nothing but death."

They made their way down a rocky slope, and Hunter could hear running water ahead. If he was right, Uncle Rick was leading them down toward a shallow ravine that hooked around to the base of Split Rock Falls. Both Hunter and his uncle had explored this land since they were very young.

"We call hunting a sport, the way we call basketball a sport, but I think that's wrong," Uncle Rick said quietly. "Basketball is fun, sure. But win or lose, not much has changed. With hunting, we hold life or death in our hands. And that's not a matter for cheers or pep music."

"But isn't this fun?" Annette whispered. "I'm not even really hunting, and I'm having fun."

It was just light enough for Hunter to see Uncle Rick shake his head. "It's enjoyable, fun maybe, but a very different kind of fun, more an excitement, something ancient, primal. It's the hunters that get out here all careless, acting like this is the Super Bowl and forgetting the deadly power they're carrying, the people who call themselves hunters who don't respect the animals, nature, or the hunt itself, who not only risk giving hunters a bad reputation, but end up getting people hurt."

"I took the hunter safety course," Hunter said.

"That was a class," said Uncle Rick. "Nobody gets hurt in a class. This is real. We need to respect the hunt."

"Come on," Annette whispered.

Hunter squeezed his rifle as they slowly made their way out into the small clearing before Split Rock Falls. It was a small stream spilling between the fissure and tumbling over rounded stones down the slope, and in the near-darkness it was hard to see. Instead he heard it, smelled it, almost felt it. The strange tricky light between night and morning could easily fool the eyes, and Hunter thought he kept seeing movement out in the shadows among the tall pines. He leaned forward for some reason, as though that would help him focus on whatever might be out there. This was, after all, where he and Yumi had seen that enormous buck. Hunter wasn't dumb enough to think he was still out here, waiting around for years for Hunter to kill him.

But that's what made this so much fun, or so enjoyable, or however Uncle Rick wanted him to think about this. They might find a massive buck. They might find nothing. They might find a giant herd of deer. Or a bear. Anything could happen in hunting. Anything at all.

Uncle Rick took a knee next to him. "Got something?" he whispered.

"I thought I saw movement," Hunter said.

Annette crouched down too, a little closer, Hunter thought, than was necessary. He tried not to notice.

"Is there something out there?" she whispered eagerly.

Uncle Rick held his finger to his lips and slowly worked the bolt action on his rifle. Hunter watched him do it, amazingly in perfect silence. Handle flip, pull back, push forward, and handle down. Uncle Rick's rifle was chambered and ready. They remained that way, motionless and silent in the early morning half-light, for a long ten minutes.

"It's OK," Uncle Rick finally whispered. "Better too alert than not enough."

The three of them continued onward toward the South Ridge gap.

A coyote scurried off into the low brush. Hunter watched its bushy tail fleeing and wished so much he could shoot it. At this range, he'd never miss, and coyotes were the worst. They even came all the way into town. Two years ago, two coyotes had attacked and killed his friend Barett Wilson's old dog when the dog was out at night peeing. That's why Barett always wished any hunter luck killing coyotes. He hated them. Hunter did too.

They continued down the slope, working their way along the

narrow trail, careful to step around all sorts of animal droppings. Uncle Rick led the way, stopping from time to time and pointing at poop for the other two to step over. Hunter could identify each different mess. It was an important skill for a hunter, helping to identify what animal had been that way, and if it had been there recently or not.

There were coyote turds, like dog poop. Raccoon logs with more seeds. Tiny round rabbit pellets.

"What?" Annette asked, surprised as they moved around a big pile of brown turd pellets, each about the size of the average gumball.

"Moose," Hunter whispered.

Three raccoons ran off up the slope toward the direction from which the human intruders had come. Hunter and Uncle Rick exchanged a silent look of surprise. The raccoons were huge! Biggest Hunter had ever seen, larger than an overweight cocker spaniel. Raccoons looked cute and cuddly, but they were a constant nuisance, messing with garbage cans and pooping all over the tower deer stand the family used in bow hunting season. Corner one, and it could rip your face off.

As the light came up, the vague darkness before them solidified out of the inky black into the impressive cliff, and they could at last see the gap in the South Ridge. The trees thinned out a little among all those rocks on the upslope. It was the perfect position to set up. From the gap they had overwatch coverage on the whole bowl before the ridge.

Uncle Rick smiled and pointed. Then he stopped and

crouched, his rifle slung, reaching down toward the ground and picking up a brown poop pellet. "Deer," he whispered, dropping the poop.

Annette looked at him like he was crazy, her lip curled in disgust as she looked at the pile of droppings.

Uncle Rick explained in a whisper. "This crap is warm. A few hours old at most." He smiled and pointed to several different sets of hoofprints. "They're out here. Might be a good day. Come on."

"Try to move quietly," Hunter whispered to Annette. "Step onto your heel and roll your foot forward to try to avoid snapping twigs and stuff."

Annette nodded, writing in her blue notebook.

Uncle Rick smiled at Hunter and winked. Hunter's cheeks felt hot. He was glad Annette seemed to be busy writing, and hoped she hadn't noticed.

They reached the gap, a saddle formation, rather than a sharp crack or canyon, with steep smooth slopes rising from both sides to the top of the ridge. It almost divided the South Ridge into two separate formations, and was obviously the easiest way through, but it sat up high enough to make it the perfect place to shoot.

They found a place on the north side of the saddle, facing the direction from which they'd come. A pair of boulders there would provide concealment, and there was enough room behind them to prepare to shoot. One of the rocks was huge. Uncle Rick leaned forward against it, his elbows and rifle supported on top of it.

"I'll shoot from here," he said quietly.

Hunter lowered himself on his belly and low-crawled to the side of the smaller boulder nearby. There he had concealment behind the rock, but could scan the entire bowl in front of them and fire from a prone position.

At the back of the space behind the rocks, Annette took a seat on the perfect low stone shelf, which served as an ancient little bench. "What do we do now?"

"A lot of hunting, maybe most of it, involves waiting," said Uncle Rick. "It takes a lot of patience."

"This seems like a nice spot," Annette said. "Not quite as cold here behind the rocks."

Hunter looked over their morning camp. Now it was light enough to see everything clearly, and yet, at least initially, he sensed, rather than saw, its presence. Like a vibration on a tight wire, his attention sprang into focus and he saw movement at the corner of his vision. There! A deer. Coming toward them from behind, just rising over the highest point in the saddle. His heart leapt for a moment, and his hand moved to the handle of his rifle's bolt action. A second later, Hunter recognized it as a doe.

"Don't move," Uncle Rick whispered. "If we get busted, if she spots us, she'll snort to warn off any others."

"Maybe we should hide behind the rocks?" Annette whispered.

"Any movement will give us away," Hunter hissed.

The three of them froze there, watching the deer reach down to nibble at some scrub brush by a rock. Then her head came up, she straightened her neck to push her nose forward, and sniffed.

Hunter remained still. He barely blinked. He fought to keep his chest from moving too much when he breathed. Did she have their scent? There wasn't much of a breeze, but it was blowing in her direction. He hoped that all their care in washing their clothes and showering with de-scenting detergent and shampoo would be worth it. The deer turned and looked back the way she had come. Hunter took that moment to back up into their little camp, the better to avoid being busted. He crouched down and the other two did as well. It was a risk, but if that deer continued through the saddle she'd walk right past them, and as exposed as they had been, it was impossible that she would fail to notice them. Finally the doe walked on by. She was just a little thing, maybe a year old, maybe good to eat in a few years.

The three of them settled in to wait. But for Hunter it wasn't like waiting at the dentist's office when his phone was out of a charge or sitting through study time waiting for the clock to run out when all his work was done. Out here in nature, there was no hurry, no pressure to keep an online conversation going, no worries about whether or not someone liked his post or if he was supposed to click "like" on a friend's post. No school bell to tell him when to get up and move and when he should be in his seat. Out in the woods, there was only the purpose, the hunt, the sun shining down on the most perfect, untouched wilderness, and the eager expectation for taking an animal.

Hunter found himself enjoying letting his thoughts wander. He noticed Annette apparently doing the same thing, writing in her blue notebook. What was she writing? What did she think of the day so far? What did she think of him?

She seemed to notice him watching just then, and she looked up and smiled. Then her eyes widened and focused above him. She pointed. An enormous bald eagle had launched from a tree about twenty yards away, so close they could see its talons, hear the whisper of wind when it flapped its wings. It circled around and around, gliding on the air as if by magic. Then, with its sharp talons out, it plummeted to the ground. Wings flapped frantically in the grass for a few seconds until it beat its way back into the air, gripping the still-twitching form of a snake.

Annette watched wide-eyed, then mimed shooting the bird. Hunter shook his head. She shrugged and offered him a questioning look. He opened his mouth to explain, but Uncle Rick pressed a finger to his own lips, warning him to be quiet, pointing two fingers at his eyes before pointing out at the land they were supposed to be watching. Hunter did as his uncle suggested, but after a minute Annette handed him her blue notebook turned to a fresh page, her pen clipped to the cover.

On an otherwise blank page was written: *It would look great on the wall next to Reagan the Bear.*

Hunter grabbed the pen and wrote: *Illegal to kill eagles or mess with their nests. Big fine. Protected.* He handed back the notebook. She sat down next to him, read his message, and wrote back.

I know! I was just teasing you.

Hunter replied, *Got me. You're the smartest girl in our whole grade.*

It was like texting, with paper and pen.

Annette answered, *Thanks. You're sweet.*

Hunter had no idea what to write. He sat there like an idiot, staring at the paper. Fortunately, Annette took the notebook back and wrote more. *I think this is super neat. You're so cool being able to do this.*

He wasn't sure he would be able to do this when the time came. He looked away. He was supposed to be keeping a lookout for deer anyway, not paper-texting. Out near where the doe had passed, Hunter saw, in a patch of mud, a set of tracks. He frowned. At first he thought they were raccoon prints, but these were too big. And raccoon prints had five clawed fingers, sometimes appearing as if they were made by a small human hand. These were more like dog prints, with four clawed fingers and a center pad.

Hunter tapped his uncle and pointed at the prints. They all risked walking over there to look.

Dog? Annette wrote.

Hunter took the notebook. *Coyote?*

Uncle Rick shook his head. He poked his finger into the wet

earth in the middle of the print. Then he took the notebook. *Wolf prints*, he wrote. *Fresh.*

Are we in danger? Annette wrote, looking all around them. Hunter and Uncle Rick also surveyed the area.

Uncle Rick wrote next. *We're safe. Wolves cover ground very fast. It's probably long gone by now. I've only seen a wolf out here on this land one time. Years ago.*

Hunter and Annette patiently waited for Uncle Rick to finish writing, and they both felt better having read his words. Still, the idea that wolves might be out here, might have come through this very area only last night, prodded Hunter's adrenaline, filled him with an excitement, a sense of fear, and a reminder that this was all real. He held his gun a bit tighter.

He should have spotted those wolf prints as soon as they reached their position. Instead he'd been messing around watching the eagle and writing notes with Annette. He would focus now. He exchanged glances with Uncle Rick, who looked about, as if searching for the wolf, before shrugging and smiling, like it was all no big deal. That's what he loved about Uncle Rick. A warrior. A fearless man. And powerful. He always knew how to help Hunter.

Hunter rolled into the prone position beside his rock again and waited. Hoping, praying, *willing* the deer to come through their sector. He fought to keep from wondering if Kelton Fielding had taken a deer yet. He tried to stop worrying about Yumi and Uncle Rick. Above all, he forced himself not to think about what Annette had meant when she had called him sweet.

A couple of times he spotted movement and for a moment his heart leapt, but it turned out to be another raccoon and later two squirrels chasing each other around.

Then he heard the loud snap of a twig, saw the lower branches of a pine shake a little, and there at the far edge of the bowl, a fine big buck emerged from the woods. Oh, he was big, and moving slowly toward them, starting up the slope toward the gap. Another, smaller buck and three does were with him, one of the does skittish, checking behind her and trotting a little before slowing down and checking again. Had Grandpa, Dad, and Yumi pushed this little herd right here?

It was perfect. Hunter already had a round in the chamber. He eased the safety off. The weapon was ready to fire.

Hunter sensed now, could feel somehow, that the other two were watching, well aware of the opportunity before them. Uncle Rick was a great shot, and from his position, with that McMillan TAC-338, he couldn't miss. Hunter risked a look up at his uncle, who smiled before he gave a gentle head nod like, *You take the shot.*

Here it was, then. This was the big time. Hunter's moment. He probably could have shot the buck already, but as long as it was still approaching, he'd let it move a little closer, the easier to score a solid clean kill shot. Hunter's heart beat so loudly, he worried the deer would hear and take off running.

The buck was magnificent. Hunter scanned its rack. Unbelievable. It couldn't be—that was impossible. The Phantom? But how many perfect ten—No! It was bigger than that. Yumi had been right. It was a twelve-by-twelve. Twenty-four total points, and two of those were drop tines! Two perfect drop tines pointing downward. He was enormous. Powerful. Beautiful.

Hunter brought his rifle stock to his cheek and closed his left eye. He peered through his scope, centering crosshairs over where he'd have to hit to pierce the deer's heart.

He had to control his breathing so the natural rise and fall of his chest didn't move the rifle all over. A few deep breaths to try to calm down. Then he breathed in—and out—and in.

Finger on the trigger.

And he breathed out.

Just pull the trigger! Hunter screamed at himself inside his head. *Shoot it! You can't miss from here! Shoot it!*

He watched the incredible animal, the kind of buck that would be family legend for years to come. How many years of hunting had the buck survived? No humans had taken it. It had avoided wolves. It was the kind of perfect majestic beast whose picture belonged on the cover of outdoor magazines.

Shoot it! Don't be a chicken! Don't be a loser or one of those snowflake hippie anti-hunters Grandpa is always complaining about. Please. Please shoot it!

But how could he kill a beautiful powerful wild animal? How?

The more he thought about it, the more upset he became. His breathing came on harder. He had to wipe the sweat from his eyes. He was deep in the adrenaline rush of a full buck fever, but it was hopeless.

"I can't do it," he said, lowering his head in shame.

Coward! Failure! Hippie!

When he looked back up and wiped his eyes, he could swear the buck looked right at him. It was as though even the mule deer knew Hunter was a useless disgrace to his name. It stared at Hunter and his rifle in the perfect understanding that neither posed a real threat. Then it stamped a hoof and snorted. The ears of the other deer perked up a split second before the big buck bolted along the base of the South Ridge, heading west and curving back in the general direction from which they'd come, but probably well out of the way of where the others had planned to focus their pushing efforts.

Hunter sat up and looked down at the useless rifle in his hands. No. The rifle was not useless. The gun was perfectly good. Hunter put his rifle on safe, dropped the small magazine, and pulled back the bolt to eject the round and clear the chamber. He was the useless one. He'd wanted so badly to succeed as a real hunter like the other men in his family, but when the perfect moment finally came, he'd failed completely. He hadn't even taken the shot. He had not.

CHAPTER 8

YUMI TRIED TO HIDE HER DISAPPOINTMENT. THAT WAS the problem. Yumi was trying to hide her disappointment with Hunter's cowardice, and Hunter *knew* she was trying to hide her disappointment. He would have preferred it if she yelled at him.

Come on! We worked hard making those deer move your way! How could you have missed that shot!? What's the matter with you?

Instead, after she'd more or less figured out that Hunter had had the perfect buck lined up in a perfect shot, she forced a smile. "Well," she'd said, "it can happen to anyone."

Anyone who was a coward. Hunter's rifle felt extra-heavy, hanging from its sling, weighing down his shoulder. How could this have happened?

Dad, Grandpa, and Yumi had joined them at the foot of the South Ridge, gathered around to hear the pathetic story near the place where the proud buck had stood. Hunter felt like he'd slipped into a nightmare. Except that Hunter could never get back to his own dimension, a place where he had taken the shot.

Taken the shot because he was *hunting*! Now they might never see a buck like that for years, perhaps ever.

"It's getting late," Grandpa said. "Sun's well up. The deer will be bedded down now. We'll head back to the lodge, get something to eat. Some rest. Come back out and try again at dusk."

Yumi gently pulled Annette along with her, leading the way back in the direction of the lodge, both of them whispering and sneaking pitying glances back at Hunter.

He walked slowly, to let everybody else get ahead. Dad started to hold back, but Uncle Rick coughed and cleared his throat, and Dad moved along.

The only thing worse than being too chicken to shoot that deer was how everybody treated him like a helpless pathetic baby. Except that he *was* a helpless pathetic baby.

In fourth and fifth grade, Hunter had tried wrestling, joining the McCall Youth Warrior wrestling team. He'd joined mostly because Barett Wilson was super-excited about it. Barett was good. Hunter was, well—Coach always said he "needs improvement." At tournaments at McCall and neighboring schools, Barett usually took first or second place. Hunter did not do nearly as well, though once or twice he was happy to take second. One time, while they walked dejectedly across the parking lot to Dad's truck after another particularly bad tournament, Mom put her arm around his shoulders. "Well," she said with a faltering tone of forced optimism, "at least you got fourth."

Fourth was last place. Dead last. To earn fourth place a wrestler had to lose to all of the three other wrestlers in his bracket. Mom had basically been saying, *at least you were last* or *at least you were beaten by everyone else* or *at least you were the worst.* She'd been trying to cheer him up, that eternal optimism that librarians seemed to keep on the shelf and check out as needed. She'd meant well, but the hollow encouragement had felt worse somehow.

Now Uncle Rick fell into step beside him as they walked down the sunny slope from the South Ridge, and he waited for the at-least-you-got-fourth consolation speech.

But none came. The two of them walked in relative silence. From far off in the green temple of spruce and pine came the shrill caw of a crow. The cry grew anrgier, more frantic as the two of them approached the tree line on the far side of the clearing.

"What's wrong with me?" Hunter finally whispered, more to himself than to his uncle. But sound does tricky things in the woods. Uncle Rick must have heard him.

"Nothing's wrong with you," said his uncle. "You were reluctant to kill. Nothing wrong with that at all."

"It's cowardly," Hunter said. "I'm a wimp."

"It only means you're a decent person. You understand and have respect for the power to kill." He held back a low branch for Hunter to pass by on the trail. "Some people don't have that respect. They treat killing like a cheap game, meaningless fun. Or, worse, they enjoy killing for its own sake. They like inflicting pain."

"But the whole point of what we're trying to do out here is to kill."

Uncle Rick shook his head. "No. We're trying to take an animal, for meat, and for the triumph of outsmarting and taking a clever wild animal that knows these woods and the meaning of the hunt more than we ever will. Killing is part of our method, but it is not our purpose."

Neither of them said anything for a long time. Finally, Uncle Rick must have read the look of confusion on his nephew's face, because he sighed deeply. He spoke quietly. "You know I was in the war?"

Hunter almost laughed. He'd been told Uncle Rick had been awarded a Purple Heart for being wounded in battle. He'd earned a Bronze Star Medal. Hunter had looked it up online once. The medal was awarded for heroic achievement. Of course he knew Uncle Rick had fought in the war in Afghanistan. He just didn't know anything about what Uncle Rick had done there.

His uncle stopped them beneath a mossy outcropping of rock that loomed above them, dripping wet and leaning out over the trail a little so it almost felt as if they were in a cave. "You want to know if I killed"—he paused, and then nearly spit out the next word—"people."

Mom had always told him that his uncle probably didn't want to talk about any of this, so Hunter remained silent. And then Uncle Rick talked about it.

"I hate the Taliban," he said. He looked off into the distant woods with a cold, hard fury, and Hunter noticed him pull his rifle up a little. "Not like . . . not like you hate a pop quiz at school or some kid who's been picking on you. I mean, hate that eats down deep, poisons you. Makes you burn inside. I hope you never have to experience it." He laughed a little then. "You know *Star Wars?* It's like the dark side of the Force. Hate like that, kind of takes you over a little. Only you can't choke people with the power of your mind."

Uncle Rick looked down at his rifle and continued. "I hate the Taliban. They are monsters. Pure evil. Not because they want to kill us Americans. That's war. That's fair. That's how the game is played. But—" He choked up, cursed. "Why don't they leave their own kids alone? They'd kill girls just for going to school. They terrorize their own people. I hate them. I killed fifteen of them."

Hunter couldn't hold himself back. "See? You weren't scared! You killed—"

"That's what I'm trying to tell you, Hunter! I was terrified the whole time!" Uncle Rick's voice echoed off the rocks. "Sometimes I still—" He clenched his rifle and groaned, fighting to regain control. "It isn't about courage. It's about the purpose. My purpose wasn't to kill. We were trying to get paper, pens, and other school supplies to a girls' school! I was trying to get my guys out of—" He stopped himself again.

"I could have hit that buck," Hunter said. "No problem. But I didn't because—"

"Were you scared of the buck?" Uncle Rick asked.

"No."

"Think the deer was going to hurt you?"

"Of course not. I don't—"

"So it wasn't about *fear*, Hunter. You recognized that deer as the beautiful creature that it is, and it made you recognize even more the awesome, the holy power to kill. You just need to reconcile to your purpose and choose to kill in service to that purpose.

"I absolutely hate the Taliban. But still, each one had a mother, maybe family, was a human being. If possible, I would have rather not had to kill anybody. But killing was an essential tool for my purpose at the time, and so I fired my weapon as accurately and as many times as I could. I forced myself to consciously make the choice to use that terrible power in my hands."

"What if I can't do that?" Hunter asked.

"You might not be able to," Uncle Rick said. He resumed leading the walk back toward the lodge. "Or you might not be able to kill on this hunting trip. Maybe you'll figure it out next time, or next year. You take a deer when you're darn well good and ready. Not before. My point is, your hesitation doesn't make you a coward. It doesn't make you weak or less of a man. It makes you human. It makes you a good person. Roger?"

After a long moment Hunter answered. "Roger that, Uncle

Rick." He'd said he understood and agreed, and he smiled like he felt much better. He supposed that this talk with Uncle Rick helped him a little, and he was honored that his uncle would choose to share so much with him. But Hunter still had to go back and face the rest of the family—and Annette—having just let the best buck any of them were likely to see for years walk away easy.

Despite the awkwardness from the morning, it felt good to get back to the lodge and get out of all that hunting gear, in the warm confines of the cabin. The lodge's furnace ran on propane, but in the cabin part there was also a round black woodstove in which Grandpa had a hot fire burning. The girls sat on the floor around the woodstove, Yumi with Uncle Rick's desert camo poncho liner over her shoulders, Annette draped in a woodland picture blanket with a five-by-five buck image staring right at Hunter, as if mocking him. The men were in the kitchen, having a beer and talking about the morning.

Hunter dropped onto the camo-upholstered recliner in the middle of the living room.

"Hey, Hunter," Annette said brightly. "I was just telling Yumi that I can really see the fun in this sport. I'm going to take the hunter safety course and get my license, and maybe I'll get into hunting. Of course, my thing, besides journalism and writing, is fishing. This summer maybe we can get out on Payette Lake or Payette River and catch some trout or catfish."

"That would be great," Yumi said, flashing a quick look at Hunter.

"What do you think, Hunter?" Annette said. "I know some choice fishing spots."

Hunter forced a smile and nodded. "Sure. Sounds good."

Maybe Annette was just being nice. Perhaps she really was simply enthusiastic about fishing, and eager to share her favorite outdoor sport with the two who were sharing theirs with her. Annette really was very nice. But he felt like she was offering a consolation prize, an outdoor adventure to serve as a replacement for this one at which he'd so obviously failed.

The funny thing was he'd gone fishing plenty of times. He'd caught a few fish. A twenty-two-pound salmon once that he'd hardly been able to reel in. The fish had died not long after he'd pulled it ashore. By taking it out of the water, he'd effectively killed it. And he'd had no problem with that. So what was wrong with him and deer?

It always came back to his failure with the deer.

They all ate lunch, the last of the previous year's venison steaks from the deep freeze out in the garage. For a while Grandpa, a Republican, debated with Dad, a Democrat, about some tax issue in which Hunter wasn't particularly interested. Uncle Rick, who insisted he supported no party save for the party of common sense, spoke up once in a while. Yumi and Hunter exchanged a nervous look. Sometimes these debates exploded into loud bitter arguments that only a walk or a hunt through the woods could subdue. Hunter hoped nothing like that would happen today, especially in front of Annette.

"You know, I remember a hunt," Grandpa said, finally changing the subject from politics, so abruptly that everybody listened closely, "back when I was a boy. A month before that, two boys in my grade, Eddie Mara and Bruce Callard, had been out hunting. Bruce hadn't been paying close enough attention when he shot a deer, hadn't seen Eddie way back behind the animal. The bullet severed an artery, and Eddie bled out and died. Bruce was never quite the same after that."

"I remember Bruce Callard," said Uncle Rick. "He, um, had a lot of problems."

Grandpa waved away any further discussion of Mr. Callard's trouble. "Anyhow, when I was out there hunting that fall, my buddy Josh was pushing. There I was, with the best rifle I had in those days, lined up on a perfect shot. Solid four-by-four buck. That was the big time. I was full into the buck fever. Adrenaline coursing through me. Heart pumping heavy. That sort of hyper-alert state of mind, fully in touch with the buck and the wilderness around me. But—" Grandpa took a swig of beer from his can. "I don't know what it was. It's hard to describe. The hunter's instinct. Not a literal voice, but the understanding, something telling me to stop, to wait. Something felt not quite right. The buck eventually took off out of range, and at first I thought I'd been busted, that maybe it smelled me or saw me. But a moment later Josh pushed through the shrubbery right behind where that deer had stood. If I had fired, I might have killed him, just like Bruce killed Eddie."

Hunter focused all his attention on cutting his steak, not wanting to meet anyone's eyes. Why couldn't everyone just let this go? Why hadn't he just shot the stupid deer?

"My point is, I would rather be out there with a hunter who refuses to take a thousand shots, with someone who trusts his hunter's instinct, than with someone who shoots all the time, who is reckless and might get people hurt or killed."

Hunter was glad when lunch, and the accompanying consolation lecture, was over and the Monopoly board was brought out.

"You're welcome to join us, Annette," Dad said. "But you should know this is cutthroat Monopoly. All chance, community chest, and taxes go into the middle of the board to be won by whoever lands on free parking."

Annette smiled. "That's how my family plays too."

"But we play serious," said Uncle Rick. "You have to pay attention to the properties you own."

"If you fail to notice that another player has landed on your property," Dad said in full lawyer mode, "and the next player rolls for his turn, you forfeit the rent to which you would otherwise have been entitled."

"What?" Annette frowned. "That seems harsh."

Hunter smiled. The only thing at their family gatherings more intense than the political discussions were the games of Monopoly.

Dad continued, "If you quit the game before it is over, you will be banned for life."

"That's actually true," said Yumi. "Aunt Lorie quit a Monopoly game when her and my dad and Uncle David were around, like, ten years old. She hasn't been allowed to play with them ever since."

Annette laughed, but Dad did not. "Also, there are no illegal mergers, no team-ups with other players just to complete color groups and otherwise combine assets."

Annette narrowed her eyes and nodded slowly. "I accept your challenge, Mr. Higgins."

And the game was on. Grandpa, like Hunter, liked to play the game cool and calm. They didn't gloat when landing on a great investment property, and they didn't laugh when collecting rent. Hunter thought this helped later on if he ever wanted to make a deal with another player, a trade or purchase to complete a color group. But Dad, Uncle Rick, and Yumi played it brash and bold.

"Boom!" Yumi shouted when a miraculous sequence of dice rolls managed to help her complete the purple color group in record time. "Uh-oh! Look out, everyone! Houses going up already? And with two railroads, I'm already dominating the game."

But then the dice turned. Yumi kept landing on chance, community chest, and jail. While others bought up properties, she paid taxes, fees, or scored small payments. Uncle Rick managed to pick up two massive piles of cash by landing on free parking. It wasn't long until Uncle Rick sealed some key deals and had finally bankrupted everyone else out of the game.

Dad shook his hand. Grandpa clapped and sat back in his chair with a satisfied look on his face.

"That was intense." Annette laughed. "I don't think I've ever played it quite like that before."

"That was fun," Yumi said. She forced a smile, but Hunter knew her better than anyone. Yumi was competitive. Once in a game, she hated to lose it. Maybe that explained why Hunter's failure to shoot bothered her so much. But she'd been a little better at hiding her disappointment over that. Now she stood up from the table and nodded toward Hunter and Annette, who were putting the game away. "You guys got that? I'm gonna go out and get some air."

"Sure, no problem," Annette said evenly, apparently not realizing Yumi was upset. She never went outside just to "get some air." What did that even mean? She was competitive, yeah. But she'd never basically stormed out after a loss before.

Hunter and Annette stood side by side, kind of close together, as they packed away the different denominations of fake money into the correct plastic slots. It wasn't a big deal or anything. But, once, their hands had kind of brushed together as they both reached to put back some five-hundred-dollar bills. Still, although Hunter didn't really want to leave, he needed to go see what was up with Yumi.

CHAPTER 9

WITH THE HEAD START YUMI HAD ON HUNTER, SHE COULD have been about anywhere in the woods outside the lodge, but Hunter's cousin was also his best friend. She could have gone anywhere, but he was pretty sure he knew exactly where she would be.

Back behind the lodge, over near the firing range, a strange tower of rock rose up out of the ground due to some weird geological process about a zillion years ago, mostly flat and about eight feet across on top. When Yumi was really young, she'd gone crazy about princesses. It was during this phase that Yumi had named this rock formation Princess Tower. Later, as Yumi left royalty behind in favor of sports and the outdoors, it became simply the Tower.

That's where he found her, sitting on the center stone that provided the perfect chair, her arms wrapped around her knees, which she'd pulled up to her chest, the way she had often done when she was upset as a little kid.

As Hunter approached the base of the Tower, he knew Yumi

had seen him, but she didn't say anything or really look at him. "Princess Yumi?" Hunter called up to her. "May I approach?" He was already starting his climb through a crack they always used as the way up.

"If you call me princess again, I'll knock you off the Tower."

It was a joke as lame as Hunter's had been, but her voice lacked its usual sharp fire.

"You OK?" Hunter asked when he reached the top and sat down next to her. "I haven't seen you looking so miserable up here on the Tower since your boyfriend Stuart Cassidy dumped you."

That actually made Yumi laugh, and Hunter was glad to see her smile. She put her head down on her arms folded over her knees and sighed. "You idiot. That was in fourth grade. Fourth-grade boyfriends don't count as real boyfriends. I'm not even sure if sixth-grade relationships are real." She looked up at him. "Oh, but don't tell Annette I said that."

"I don't get it," said Hunter.

"She's about as dopey as all that old princess stuff with the way she likes this secret someone."

Hunter shifted to try to find a more comfortable position on the rock. "Um, who is he?"

"I don't *know*, idiot! That's why it's called a secret." She frowned and kept watching him. "Why? Why do you care?"

"I don't," Hunter said a little too loudly. And he really didn't care. Unless he did. He shook his head. This was too complicated. Annette wasn't even supposed to *be* here! "I was just curious," he said quickly.

Yumi watched him a moment longer. "Right," she said, drawing out the word.

Hunter had come this far. He wasn't about to be sidetracked by Annette's love life. "Why do you care so much about Monopoly? We've played a lot of games. I've won most of them—"

"Um, no. You've won a very small percentage of them. I usually destroy you because you are terrible—"

"—Because I'm awesome—"

"—at Monopoly," Yumi and Hunter finished together. They laughed again.

Neither of them said anything for a long time after that.

"How can my dad have so much fun playing the game?" Yumi asked.

"Because he was winning?" Hunter tried. "That's usually fun."

"If he can do something as perfectly normal as playing Monopoly, like everything is fine, if he can laugh and have fun as though he doesn't have a care in the world . . ." Her voice wavered and grew quiet. "Then why can't—" A sob shook her. Hunter didn't know what to do, so he just put his arm around her shaking shoulders. "Why can't he come home?"

He knew it probably wasn't the type of question to which Yumi was expecting his answer, but she looked and sounded so sad that he felt like he had to say something. "Well, I think—"

"He says that it's not because of Mom or me, but why is

he only happy when he's away from us? He's more comfortable around Annette, around *you*, than being with his own *daughter*!"

"It's not like that," Hunter said.

"Then what is it *like*, Hunter!" she snarled. "He's been living out here, by himself, for over a month! Then he ... then he makes me come out here this weekend." She threw her hands up. "I flat-out told him no, but he kept pushing, and then Mom jumped in on his side, so in the end I managed to get them to cave and agree to let me bring Annette along."

Hunter put his head back and looked up to the branches. So that was why Annette had come along. Some kind of special deal to get Yumi to come out here.

"Dad tried telling me something like, 'Oh, if we go hunting together, then we'll fix things up.'" Yumi rolled her eyes. "Does he seriously believe that we'd come out to the woods and that would magically make up for the way he *abandoned* us?"

Hunter frowned. That wasn't fair. Uncle Rick was a cool guy, a hero, really. He literally had hero medals from the war.

"I don't think he abandoned you."

Yumi shot up on her feet. "Oh, then what would you call this? I can't believe you're taking his side."

"I'm not taking any side," Hunter said. "I know he loves you and stuff. I think maybe he's just having a hard time."

"Oh, like the kind of hard time where he just has fun playing Monopoly?"

Hunter frowned. "He was in a war, Yumi. He got shot and—"

"Oh, stop! I'm sick to death of hearing about the stupid war. I'm sorry. I just don't care about Afghanistan! Those people can . . ." She stopped herself and took a deep breath. "No, I don't mean that. I just . . ." Tears came again. "I just want my dad back."

"Well, maybe being out here is a chance for that," Hunter said after a long silence. "Anything can happen out here hunting."

"Or not happen." Yumi wiped her eyes. "You want to explain what happened with that deer?" She wasn't asking the question as an accusation. She didn't sound sharp or condescending. Her tone and the expression on her face were more of concern than anything else. "You're a better shooter than I am," she said after some hesitation.

Hunter knew that wasn't an easy thing for Yumi to admit. But just then he was having trouble admitting, even to himself, the real answer to her question. He opened his mouth to speak, but stopped himself, unsure how to explain this in a way she could understand, in a way anyone could understand.

"Come on, Higgins," she said. "If you're going to get all personal with me and expect me to spill on my deepest, darkest, most emotional whatever, don't think you're getting off the hook."

"I wasn't scared," Hunter said.

"Well, that's good. It was a deer, not a bear or a wolf."

"I was set up for the perfect shot. I wanted to shoot it. I've been dreaming about this hunting trip for months."

"Oh, I knooooow." Yumi picked up a small stone and whipped it with her cool sidearm throw. "It's all you've talked about since forever."

"I'm not against hunting," he said.

"Obviously."

"It's like, I wanted to shoot the deer. But also, I didn't want to kill the deer. It was too beautiful. I know hunting's not wrong, but killing it felt wrong," Hunter said. Yumi flashed him a confused look. He continued, "I know that sounds stupid. I hate myself for being such a—"

"Cool guy!" Yumi cut in quickly. "You're one of the best guys I know, Higgins. We're going back out again later today. You might still get one. And even if you don't—so what? Most hunters come back empty-handed. What's Grandpa always saying? It's not about the deer you take home, but about the experience."

"Yeah, but you never hear hunters brag about their experience."

Yumi elbowed him. "Come on, Higgins. Since when have you ever cared about bragging? You want to be like Kelton Fielding or something?"

"No." Hunter laughed. It felt good to laugh. Yumi could somehow always bring that out of him.

"Can I ask you just one thing?" Hunter did not know where the inspiration or courage to bring up this matter had come from, but before he'd really thought about it, he was speaking, and once he'd started he had to see it through. Maybe he simply remembered his father talking about how hunting had been the last thread of connection between his father and Grandpa back when the two of them were not getting along. Maybe he simply wanted to reduce the tension this weekend. Either way, he wasn't sure which was harder, killing the deer or bringing this up.

Yumi must have sensed the worry in his voice, because she looked at him warily. "Okaaaay?"

"When we go back out, come with me and Uncle Rick," Hunter said. Yumi frowned and was about to speak, but Hunter hurried on. "Just because it would be cool to be on the same team. Besides, Annette was pretty lonely, I think, with you not there."

"Oh, but surely she didn't get too lonely with *you* around!"

Hunter backed away from Yumi a little. "What are you talking about? She's *your* friend. You're the one who brought her here."

"Cut the crap, Higgins. I've noticed you looking at her."

"Yeah," Hunter said quickly. "The same way I look at you or my dad or Reagan. I mean, I have to look to know where she is, so she's not downrange of my rifle."

"That's not what I meant, and you know it," Yumi said.

"Are you two up there?" Annette called to them from below.

Hunter flashed his cousin a warning glare against her teasing smile. "Just, will you come with us or not?"

Yumi sighed. "Fine. I guess."

Yumi and Hunter made their way to the edge of the Tower and looked down to see Annette, hand up to block the sun from her eyes, smiling up at them. "There you are. Finally. I've been looking all over for you." She frowned. "How did you even get up there?"

Hunter showed her the way.

"What? Are you two hiding?" she asked with a grin. "Leave me in there with the men and their stories about ancient times?"

"Sorry," Yumi said. "It's complicated."

Annette held her hands up. "Relax. I was just joking. They're actually pretty cool. You're both from a neat family. Makes me wish I was a Higgins too!"

How did Annette keep this up? This never-ending positive attitude. That warm, friendly smile. Even her eyes seemed to sparkle.

"Wow," Annette said, surveying the area from her new height. "It's neat up here."

Hunter started to explain. "We call it the—"

"The Tower," Yumi finished for him.

"Makes sense," Annette said, finding a seat on some pine needles.

"Well, first Yumi named this the Princess Tower—"

"Oh, I *hate* you, Higgins!" Yumi interrupted.

"—because Yumi was so sure she was going to grow up to be a princess, and if she waited up here long enough, a charming prince would come rescue her or something."

Hunter and Annette laughed. Yumi pressed her lips together to keep from smiling.

"OK," Yumi fired back. "Laugh it up. But speaking of Prince Charming, why don't you tell us about this mystery boy you like so much? Who is he?"

If Hunter thought he often blushed too easily or deeply, he

realized it was nothing compared to Annette. Her cheeks and neck flared crimson.

"I'm not telling you," Annette said. "Least of all around Hunter. He'd tell!"

Hunter felt a weird twist deep inside, kind of like a more intense version of opening a present he expected to be Legos or a new video game and finding socks instead. Why should any of this bother him? He didn't care at all who Annette liked. He did not.

Hunter held his arms out and almost shouted. "Hey, I let the perfect buck get away without firing a shot! As long as we're all being really embarrassed here."

They all laughed, and the laughter allowed a little more of the sting of his failure to fade.

"You'll have another chance," Annette said. "You'll get one when we go back out hunting later today."

"I better," Hunter said. "Or else Kelton Fielding and the other guys are going to give me so much crap."

"Oh, you're right!" Annette TapTapTapped Hunter's shoulder and a tingle went up his neck. "That guy is so annoying. I'd lose my mind if I had to sit in front of him, the way he taps on your shoulder and blathers on."

"Thank you!" Hunter's voice echoed through the woods. "I'm so glad someone else understands. Miss Foudy always brings the hammer down on both of us, like I even *want* to talk to the guy."

"Teachers never seem to understand," Yumi said.

The talk continued like that, wandering from topic to topic, for a long time. Up on the Tower, out there in the deep Idaho wilderness, Hunter felt at home. And there was something else, too. Something he didn't often experience in middle school. As the three of them talked and joked, alone in their own separate wilderness castle, he felt like he belonged, that the two of them really wanted him there, that he was more than an awkward kid who wasn't always sure how to dress or act. Last year, Mom had warned him that middle school could be tough, and, being a librarian, she had recommended about half a dozen books with characters navigating the challenge. She'd been right. But up on the Tower with Yumi and Annette, Hunter dared to hope that middle school might turn out OK after all.

"Hunter!" Dad's voice echoed through the woods back toward the cliff. "Yumi! Annette! Time to come in. We're getting ready to go hunting again."

The three of them exchanged a look, and Hunter wondered if the other two thought the same about that afternoon as he did. And without another word, they started climbing back down to the ground, to start the next hunt.

CHAPTER 10

"WHAT'S UP WITH YOU?" YUMI ASKED HUNTER AS SHE hopped around in the garage trying to push her foot through the tangled-up leg of her camouflage hunting coveralls. "Big goofy smile all the sudden."

"I'm just excited to get back out there," Hunter said, slipping on his blaze-orange vest. And he was excited. Grandpa's story and his conversation with Uncle Rick had helped some after his morning failure, but his time on the Tower with Yumi and Annette had made more of a difference. It had helped him relax, to push aside, if not forget, his worries about killing. And their long conversation had helped him get past his reservations about Yumi and Annette being here in the first place. He was actually glad they had come.

He would have been a bit lonely without Annette and Yumi, and with nothing to distract him from his failure. Who knows, but if they hadn't showed up, he might have spent the whole time between hunts enduring pitying lectures from Dad, Grandpa, and Uncle Rick. Sure, the men were only trying to help, but at a certain point Hunter simply wanted to move on.

That's what this afternoon was about. Moving on. A second chance to make this right, to bring home his first trophy deer. After talking so much with the girls, he felt like he had a team, a group supporting him.

Annette was all suited up in a one-piece set of camouflage overalls, blaze-orange vest, black gloves, and a close-fitting camo stocking cap. Except for professional hunter crybabies like Timmy Ballings, hunting wasn't a fashion show, but Hunter couldn't completely push aside the thought that Annette somehow managed to look good even in the bulky gear.

She must have noticed him looking, because she flashed that smile that wrinkled her freckled nose.

Hunter quickly looked away and tried to ignore Yumi's chuckle.

He and Yumi checked over their rifles, clearing them first, and then making sure they had loaded, four-round magazines ready.

"Guns are prepped," Yumi said when they were finished.

"Notebook ready," Annette said. "Pen and backup pen ready."

Hunter and Yumi laughed.

"Is there much of a difference between the morning hunt and the evening hunt?" Annette asked. Her voice—the way she talked—changed a little when she asked questions for her newspaper story. She still sounded friendly, but she switched to a more clipped, professional tone, perhaps an imitation of reporters she had seen on TV.

Yumi shrugged. "I don't know. This is my first hunt," she said.

"Mine too," Hunter offered. "But my dad swears the deer are more active near sunset. They're basically nocturnal, he says. So it's like they're waking up to start their day, and they're more hungry and have more energy, after resting all day, to run around looking for food. He thinks by morning they're more tired, so we won't see as many of them moving all over."

"I don't quite buy it," said Yumi. "I've heard of just as many hunters who believe the opposite. I mean, sure, they're up all night, but that would make mornings their dinner and near sunset their breakfast. Most people's dinner is bigger than their breakfast. I think your dad is just going on about a lot of superstition when he talks about that." Yumi leaned closer to Annette. "A lot of hunting is about superstition and old family stories."

The men came out of the cabin into the garage part of the lodge and began to suit up. Grandpa smiled and spoke with his usual booming voice. "Who's ready for some red-hot hunting action?"

"I am!" Annette answered.

"That's the spirit," Grandpa said. "Annette, you need to get hunting-certified and get your license so you can join in the fun for real."

"I will," she said. "But I'm having a great time just taking notes on everything. This will be a great story for the newspaper."

"All right," Dad said. "Same groups as—"

"Actually, could I go with Annette and Hunter this time?" Yumi said quickly, not making eye contact with her father.

There was a moment of silence that Hunter found extremely tense. How was it possible for silence to sometimes be so much louder than speaking or even shouting?

Dad rescued them. "That's . . . that should be fine, right?"

"Sure," Grandpa said. "No law says our groups have to be evenly numbered. This isn't football."

"It's fine with me," Uncle Rick said, trying to sound casual and unimpressed in that way that made it so perfectly clear that he was thrilled Yumi would be going with him.

Hunter had to smile, watching Uncle Rick trying to hide his grin as he finished suiting up.

"All right, then," said Grandpa, pulling his worn old hunting cap with the silly-looking ear flaps down onto his head. "Rick, your group will set up in the same place as this morning. David and I may push from another area. There are some other hot spots for deer I've seen on my trail cams. We may check them out, try to send the deer your way. But regardless, we'll make sure to stay well out of your shooting range."

"Still, make sure you have a clean, safe shot," Dad said.

"Absolutely," Grandpa agreed. "Safety is most important. Always." He didn't say anything for a moment as he drew in a deep breath through his nose, letting it out in a satisfied sigh the way a man might do upon finishing a big delicious meal. "Well, here we go again. What we have to do this afternoon is let the morning hunt, and let everything else, go. A hunter needs to be fully present. If he's too concerned with past successes or failures or if his mind is on paying the bills or whatever else from life, he'll be distracted, and he might miss that crucial moment." Grandpa looked from one person to another, gesticulating with his hands as he spoke, excited, fully into all of this. "If you're thinking about some faraway thing when you're out there, you might miss a subtle movement out in the shrubbery that will clue you in on where the deer are. You might fail to get your rifle ready in time, miss the perfect chance. That's what's great about hunting. It's just us, right here and now, out in nature, in a contest against some of the smartest, fastest, most skilled navigators of wilderness possible. For the time that we're hunting, everything else—all the frustrations and bull crap from the outside world doesn't matter." The man smiled. "So what do you say? You ready to hunt?"

A little shiver went up Hunter's back, and he nodded, trying—and mostly succeeding—to push back the doubts that had plagued him this morning. The situation was different now. He'd had more time to think and prepare himself for the kill, and he was heading out into the woods with a group more tightly knit as friends than they had been before. Dad had said hunting was about family and friends. If that was true, then he was better equipped than ever to succeed on his second try at his first hunt, and he did not worry about how he would bring himself to kill a living creature. He did not.

Once, his father had surprised him by taking him to a

Seahawks game in Seattle. The team had done poorly in the first half, giving up two fumbles and failing to get a decent offensive drive going.

"Well, maybe they'll do better in the second half," Dad had said.

Hunter doubted that very much. How could a team that had punted more than anything else suddenly start scoring and putting up a good defense? But after halftime the Seahawks seemed like a different team. They completed some great passes on their first series, and their defense quickly regained possession of the ball.

"Sometimes halftime can change everything for the better," Dad had said.

The day's hunting halftime had energized their whole crew, and Hunter was eager to get through it. This was how this trip was supposed to feel, how he had always hoped it would be.

They agreed that Uncle Rick's team would leave the lodge about twenty minutes before Grandpa and Dad. After all, if they weren't set up, the whole plan didn't make much sense. Unlike the dark morning, Hunter emerged into bright sunlight, walking in the middle of the group, following Uncle Rick south.

Yumi had started out up front with her father, and Hunter thought he noticed Uncle Rick walking a little taller, a hint of a smile on his face. Uncle Rick wasn't very good at hiding his delight in hanging out with Yumi again. She even playfully bumped her shoulder into him as they walked. He gently bumped her back.

About ten minutes later, Yumi fell back, joining Hunter and Annette five yards behind Uncle Rick, who merely nodded and winked at her.

Yumi shrugged with a satisfied smile as she walked back to her friends, looking like some kind of action hero combat girl with her camo gear and rifle. Although she hadn't said so, Hunter could tell that at least some of the anger and resentment that had plagued her when she arrived at the lodge had melted away. A lot could be communicated without words, just in the way someone walked or carried her gun.

The path upon which Uncle Rick led them went to the top of a high hill. They probably took this same route in the morning, but the predawn darkness had hidden the world. Now all four of them stopped for a moment to take in the scene. Before them stretched a breathtaking view of Idaho's wilderness. Tall spruce and pine trees and the Payette River beyond them. Another stretch of woods carpeted the land all the way to the high mountains in the distance. A couple of hawks or eagles glided on the breeze, circling in the far distance. They were so high on this hill that Hunter almost felt as though he flew with the birds, like them also seeking prey.

Annette put her hand on Hunter's arm, and a tingle shook through him. But his senses sharpened a moment later when he saw why she wanted his attention. It was hard to see, but at the far base of the hill, nibbling at a patch of raspberry bushes, were three deer, one of them a small buck.

Uncle Rick's rifle was equipped with a powerful scope.

Slowly, very slowly, he raised his gun so he could take a better look. After a moment, he slung his rifle and then held up two fingers on each hand before pointing at the deer.

This was a little two-by-two buck. Uncle Rick motioned everyone closer. When they'd huddled up, he whispered, "He's a little thing. It's up to you. But, you fill your deer tag with this smaller deer, you might have to give up a bigger, better buck later in the season. The Phantom may still be out here somewhere."

"What would you do?" Annette whispered.

"If it was the last day of the season, maybe I'd consider taking this deer. But probably not. Let him get a little bigger. We'll never have good trophy deer if we keep harvesting the young ones."

Annette was writing fast in her notebook. "How long until this one is ready?"

"About four or five years," Uncle Rick answered.

"What do we do?" Hunter said. "If we go down there and those deer bust us, they might spook out other deer. There might be a bigger buck with them."

"We'll have to wait," Yumi said. "We could hide in these bushes over here."

"But we have to get to the South Ridge," said Annette. "We need to be there when the other team pushes the deer through."

"It won't do us any good if we push the deer away from our area on the way there," Hunter said. "We have to wait. Maybe we'll end up shooting from right here. What do you think, Uncle Rick?"

Uncle Rick nodded, and that settled it. Very slowly, the four of them moved to the bushes Yumi had pointed out, and despite the thorns, they took cover there, waiting for the deer below to move on.

There was a greater sense of urgency to the hunt now, and Hunter thought the rest of his group felt it too. They were supposed to be on the South Ridge. That's where the deer drive would push the deer. Being stuck where they were, they might miss the big rush that Grandpa and Dad would be stirring up.

Annette whispered close to his ear. Hunter tried to keep focused on the hunt. "How will we know when we can move on?" she breathed.

He shrugged and turned to whisper in her ear. "Not sure. I guess we wait awhile after they've moved on. Hope for the best."

Hunter lowered himself to his belly and mimed to Uncle Rick how he planned to low-crawl to the edge of the shrubs so he could look down on the deer below. His scope wasn't as powerful as Uncle Rick's, but he didn't need to see everything down there with super-detail. He just needed to know when the deer had left, so they could get through.

If there was one thing Hunter had learned growing up in a family so interested in hunting, it was that deer were strange creatures. Except for young fawns, which sometimes chased one another around playing, deer spent their entire lives seeking food or trying to mate. And a buck tries to impress does in the dumbest ways, by rubbing the bark off part of a tree with his antlers or scratching at a patch of ground with his hooves. As

Hunter watched the deer down below, he realized there were five or six instead of the three they'd initially spotted. They were nibbling and very slowly moving west.

"This is gonna take forever," Hunter whispered. But he was wrong. A few minutes later, the young buck forgot the shrub he was eating, and his head shot up straight, big ears twitching. He looked to the east and snorted. The other deer stopped eating as well. In the next instant, they all bolted west. Not a walk or a casual trot, but a full bounding run, that peculiar fast bouncing, front and back legs working as sets, not alternating as when the creature walked. *Boing, boing, boing,* the animals bounced away, part running, part flying, scared away by something.

Hunter rejoined the others, motioning everyone to move in close. "Something scared them off."

"They get our scent?" Uncle Rick whispered.

"I don't think we were busted," Hunter breathed.

"How can you tell?" Annette asked, pen ready at her notebook.

"I don't know," Hunter admitted. "They were looking off to the east. Frozen. Then bolted the other way."

"It doesn't always make sense what they do," Uncle Rick whispered. "Let's get going."

The sun was low in the west. Hunter guessed they had two or maybe three hours of daylight left. He hoped it would be enough. The four of them went down the hill, a rocky slope with only a few trees. In the valley beyond the shrubs the passage narrowed as they walked beneath the mossy rock outcropping again.

Hunter remembered his time here with Uncle Rick this morning, how his uncle had talked about the Army. He wondered if this kind of silent stalking with guns was what it felt like to serve in a war. His only war now was against his own reluctance to pull the trigger when his moment came. If his moment came.

They finally reached the position in the South Ridge gap where they'd stood this morning, and they settled in.

"Now we wait," Yumi whispered.

"It seems like a lot of hunting is waiting," Annette said.

"The Army's even worse," said Uncle Rick, scanning their range with the rifle's scope. "Sometimes we'd hurry to get someplace, and then sit around waiting for days. For orders, for supplies, for transport."

Yumi perked up, listening intently to Uncle Rick talk. Hunter wondered how much he'd told her about his Army experiences. Now that Hunter thought about it, he realized he didn't know much about anything Uncle Rick had done in the Army or the war. He'd only heard bits and pieces. Their talk this morning was the most his uncle had told him, and that was nothing about what he'd actually done or what had happened to him.

"What's the longest you ever had to wait in the Army?" Yumi whispered, pretending to pick at a speck of nonexistent dirt on her rifle, but sneaking eager glances at her father.

"Oh," said Uncle Rick. "Hard to say."

"Sure." Yumi's shoulders fell.

"When we first pushed out to establish our FOB, our forward operations base, in Helmand Province we had a compound with high walls and guard towers, but our tactical vehicles hadn't come in yet. We had some light Toyota pickups. For about three weeks we did nothing but wait for our MRAPs, kind of armored trucks, to finally come in so we could run missions."

"What kind of missions?" Yumi asked.

"What?" Uncle Rick frowned. "Oh . . . well. You know, let's just concentrate on the deer for now."

Yumi sighed, "Yeah. Sure."

Uncle Rick looked at Yumi and was about to say something when Annette's eyes widened and she nodded to the north. Out there in the clearing, about twenty yards up the slope toward their ridge, was a big buck.

CHAPTER 11

IT WASN'T THE TWELVE-BY-TWELVE PHANTOM, BUT HE was a solid five-by-five.

"A nice buck for your first kill," Uncle Rick whispered to Hunter. "Want to give it another try?"

Annette smiled excitedly. Yumi motioned at the deer impatiently like, *Hurry up and take the shot already.*

This was it. A second chance. A real nice deer. Great rack. The buck reached down to nibble at some grass, and Hunter took that moment to slowly lower himself to the prone. Once again, he was in the perfect position for a shot.

He set his scope's crosshairs right over the animal's heart and slowed his breathing to keep the weapon from jerking around. As quietly as he could, he worked the bolt action to chamber a round, and turned off the safety.

The buck took two steps to Hunter's right. No problem. They weren't busted. He had this. He did. *Just stay right there. Don't move.*

Hunter slipped his fingertip over the trigger. He watched as the buck raised his head, standing at his full height, his proud antlers high above him. Hunter could almost feel the animal's heartbeat.

"OK," Hunter whispered. He controlled his breathing. In and out. In and out. In and . . . out. He should have shot. He lowered his rifle and wiped his face, rubbed his eye. Now he'd shoot it. Now he'd kill it.

But he couldn't. Hunter lowered the rifle again. He felt a cold dread twisting inside him.

Maybe he was overthinking this. Maybe if he didn't think, but quickly pulled the trigger. Just shoot without thinking. It was a good safe shot. Nobody was behind the deer or anything. He brought the rifle stock to his cheek and sighted the animal again. He just had to shoot.

The crack of a rifle!

The buck jerked for a moment, his head thrown up, and bolted west toward the tree line. A dark red spurt of blood arched from his side and he ran in that bouncing, bounding way deer have, but now this buck ran with a bit of a stagger, an awkward interruption to the deer's usual grace brought on by pain.

Hunter watched it all, full of a combination of surprise, horror, and pity. By the standards he'd seen on all those hunting videos, it was a good, clean shot. A quick kill.

"Nice shot," Uncle Rick said aloud. "Wow. Great job."

Hunter put his rifle on safe, then dropped his magazine and pulled the bolt back to eject his round. "But Uncle Rick, I didn't even—" He turned around and froze.

Standing right beside him, Yumi lowered her rifle and smiled. She cranked back the bolt and ejected her spent round casing. The casing for the bullet that had brought down the trophy buck that he'd been unable to kill.

He felt himself shaking with a crushing mix of anger and shame. Why hadn't he just shot the thing? The sense of camaraderie he'd felt that afternoon on the tower was gone, replaced with outrage and disappointment. Yumi had betrayed him. If she'd only given him a moment more, maybe he would have dropped that buck himself.

"Great shot, kid!" said Uncle Rick. Yumi and her father high-fived, but then he pulled her into a hug. He wasn't bothering to keep quiet now. "Amazing!"

Hunter hadn't moved. He remained on the ground, looking back at his cousin openmouthed.

"What?" she finally said. "He was about to bolt. I was worried you weren't going to shoot."

"I was gonna," Hunter said a little too sharply. He was trying to conceal his disappointment.

"Well, soooorry!" Yumi snapped. "I didn't understand this was the everybody-sit-and-wait-for-Hunter-to-be-the-only-shooter-type hunting party."

"Hey, hey, easy, now," said Uncle Rick. "The point is someone in our party shot that deer."

"Exactly!" Annette said. "But he's getting away!"

Uncle Rick laughed. "I don't think he'll get very far."

"But shouldn't we be running to go get him?" Annette looked

anxiously in the direction the buck had run. "How will we find him? He's deep in the woods now."

Uncle Rick started walking down the slope from the ridge. "We don't want to follow too closely and bump him up now that he's been shot. The more tense the deer is, the less he'll bleed. This isn't like football. We aren't going to tackle him. The more closely we pursue, the more likely we'll lose him. We're hoping he goes away, but not too far, thinks he's safe, and beds down to bleed out. If we're right on his tail, he'll keep running and die much farther away. We'll wait awhile and then head in the direction he went and try to pick up his blood trail."

"We're really going to track the deer by its blood?" Annette asked.

"From here on out, this all gets pretty gory," Uncle Rick said. "That's just part of it."

Yumi and Uncle Rick talked over her shot, discussing where she'd hit the deer, how she'd aimed, what a great trophy the deer would make. Annette asked eager questions, and a few times she squeezed Yumi in an excited one-armed hug.

Hunter tried not think about how the celebration should have been for the deer he took. He tried not to think about how Annette's congratulatory hug should have been for him. He did not think of these things. He did not.

And Yumi was Hunter's cousin and best friend. He shouldn't be mad at her. They'd hung out together since they were babies. But then why had she stolen this deer from him? She'd known how much this meant to him. He'd been talking about this hunting trip for weeks. They'd discussed it just this afternoon up on the tower.

Worse than the fact that she'd stolen his deer was the fact that she was right. It wasn't *his* deer. Today wasn't all about him. And he had been stalling out again, unable to shoot. Reluctant to kill. And Yumi had nailed that sucker with a great shot. Wasn't it better that the group went home with something rather than turning up empty-handed?

No. It wasn't better. On Monday Kelton Fielding would tap Hunter on the shoulder and ask in that snide mocking voice he had, *Hey, Hunter, did you take a deer this weekend?* If his family had all come back without taking a deer, he could tell Kelton that. There was no shame in it. It happened to tons of hunters all the time.

But now he'd feel that horrible TapTapTap and Kelton would be like, *Hey, Hunter, I heard Yumi shot a buck for you. Too scared, huh? Had to have a girl kill a deer for you?* Kelton wouldn't stop there. He'd get all the other hunting kids in on it too.

The guys would light him up for this. Hunter wanted to punch something, to scream at the world.

After about half an hour the four of them walked down the slope from the South Ridge, heading west in the direction the wounded deer had run, toward the point where it had vanished into more dense woods. When they reached the tree line the deer was nowhere in sight. Uncle Rick pointed to a large splash of blood dripping from a low shrub. "You can usually tell within the first hundred yards if he's bleeding good enough to keep going or if we need to back off and give him more time."

Uncle Rick was whispering now, looking around the ground for blood.

"*Psst.*" Hunter signaled the others and crouched to point at a patch of dark red blood, like paint, on a bed of pine needles. A few drips trailed away from the patch in a northwest direction.

Uncle Rick checked it out, smiled, and patted Hunter on the back. Hunter pointed in the direction of the drips, and Uncle Rick nodded. Hunter almost smiled. A bit of the excitement, the buck fever, was returning as he helped track the buck, even if he hadn't shot the thing.

But just because the pursuit was exciting didn't mean it was easy. It was a solid forty yards before they found more blood. They fanned out as they hiked up another slope. Just as Hunter began to worry they'd lost the trail, that maybe they were going to leave a wounded animal suffering in the woods, he saw another splash of blood on a rock. He gave a little whistle for the others, and by the time they'd gathered, he'd noticed disturbed pine needles and dirt and hoofprints heading in a more western direction from that point.

"That's good," Uncle Rick whispered. "He's bleeding real solid." He took a few more steps in the direction of the tracks, noticing more blood on a low tree branch. He motioned for the others to follow.

Now the group took big steps, and faster, barely avoiding the temptation to run, eager to find the buck Yumi had wounded.

Suddenly Uncle Rick dropped like a rock to the forest floor, groaning in pain. He bit his lip to muffle a curse, curling up on his side around his rifle and gripping his ankle.

"What happened?" Yumi was on her knees beside him in an instant.

"Stepped in—" He gritted his teeth against the pain. "Rabbit hole or something."

Uncle Rick rolled to sit up, still wincing in pain.

"Should we call for help?" Annette asked. "Anyone have a first-aid kit?"

"No, no." Uncle Rick grunted. "I'm fine." He pushed himself onto the knee of his good leg, and then started to stand.

"Dad, maybe you shouldn't try to—"

Uncle Rick grimaced and fell again. He laughed a little. "Oh man, does that hurt. This is stupid." His eyes watered.

"We gotta go for help," Yumi said. "We'll find Grandpa and Uncle Dave."

"No," said Uncle Rick. "We'll lose the trail."

"But you're hurt," Yumi began.

"I don't think it's broken. Twisted or sprained." Uncle Rick squinted his eyes. "Not life-threatening. I'm fine. Now, listen. You kids go on ahead. Like we've been doing. Find one spot of blood or deer tracks, then look for the next."

"I'm not leaving you alone out here." Yumi folded her arms.

"It's like the Army soldier's creed I read. 'I will never leave a fallen comrade.'"

Uncle Rick smiled. "This is Idaho, not Afghanistan."

"You can't make me leave you here," Yumi said.

"We can't leave an animal that we wounded out there in the woods!" Uncle Rick said roughly.

"Me and Annette can track the deer. You two stay," Hunter said.

For a moment Hunter thought he saw a hot look of anger from his cousin. Was she mad at him? Did she think he was trying to take her trophy deer? But then she nodded her agreement.

"Go," Yumi said. "We'll catch up if we can."

Uncle Rick signaled a thumbs-up. "Good luck."

Hunter flashed a curious look at Annette.

She shrugged and smiled. "Let's go get that deer."

CHAPTER 12

HUNTER AND ANNETTE WALKED OFF IN THE DIRECTION
they could best figure according to the blood and the tracks.
Every few yards, Hunter looked back, both to check on Uncle
Rick and to make sure he was still traveling the right direction
from the last sign of the deer's course.

They walked on through a pass between two gray boulders.
Quiet. Alert for any movement.

"Hunter!" Annette hissed, pointing to a dark spot about five
yards ahead on a flat rocky patch of ground.

The two of them hurried up to the point. There was a lot
more blood there than at the last places they'd seen it. It wasn't
puddled as much as before. Part of the blood was smeared,
and dirt and small rocks were scraped around. The buck had
stumbled here. With no experience tracking, Hunter had no
idea how much farther the buck would go. But he was bleeding
a lot, and Hunter was certain he had fallen here. Surely the buck
would die soon.

"Which way now?" Annette asked.

Hunter didn't know. There didn't seem to be any hints about the direction the deer had taken.

He broke a branch on a shrub near the new blood spot. That would let him be able to keep track of the location so they could come back to this point on the trail if they lost it. "Let's circle around from here. Watch for other broken branches, hoofprints, or more blood."

He and Annette split up to check the area around the last blood spot he'd marked, but though he looked carefully, and for what felt like a long time, there was no other sign of the buck. He worried they may be losing the deer. He was certain they were losing daylight. Once the sun went down, the buck was gone.

He and Annette agreed to widen their search area, looking for clues up to thirty yards from the place he'd marked. Still nothing. The low sun was shining in their eyes and casting long shadows. Had the change in the light affected his ability to find the right clues?

This was no good. He needed to make progress, and soon. He stopped scanning the ground around him and surveyed the broader area. If he, Hunter, had been shot, and was trying to run away, where would he go?

"Downhill would probably be easier," he whispered.

"What?" Annette hissed, rejoining him.

"If he's hurt, maybe he doesn't want to waste energy going uphill. Maybe he'd go downhill."

"And maybe he'd look for cover," Annette said. "Try to hide in that thicker brush down there."

Hunter looked at her, not hiding anything anymore, not trying to act tough or as if he knew what he was doing. "Maybe. I hope so. Come on."

They were rewarded fifty yards later when they spotted a big splash of blood. Annette was almost jumping as she put her hand on his forearm, smiling brightly. A trail of blood drips led them in the direction they'd both guessed before, and the two of them hurried off about as fast as they could while still being safe. You had to be careful running with a rifle in hand.

More blood on a decently worn deer trail. Some fresh deer pellets. Hunter led Annette down a narrow path through thick brush.

He froze. She bumped into his back. And slowly, very slowly, Hunter crouched down to the forest floor, Annette right behind him.

About thirty yards ahead of them, lying in his own blood on a bed of thick dry grass, his head drooped a little, was the buck Yumi had shot.

A new energy surged in Hunter, as he'd at last found their prey. He'd made up, at least in part, for his pathetic inability to shoot the animal. If he hadn't tracked the deer, they'd have lost it for sure. Now when people looked at this buck's head on the wall and told the story about how it was taken, he'd at least be part of the team effort that brought it in.

Slowly, quietly, Hunter crept closer. He could see the animal's pain, his heavier breathing, big huffs through his nose, blood matting down his side. A slight trembling in his legs.

"There are bubbles in his blood," Hunter whispered to Annette, not to avoid scaring the deer away, for the fight had bled out of him now, but out of respect for the buck. "Different signs in the blood give different clues about where the deer was hit. Looks like Yumi scored a lung shot."

Somehow the buck understood Hunter was here, fixing him in his big, blank, black-eyeball gaze. Hunter worried for a moment that he'd ruined everything, alerting the deer to send him running away to vanish into the night. But this buck was done running. He'd never get up again.

His eyes met Hunter's, and without thinking, Hunter stood and stepped closer to the wounded animal. The deer watched him, and seemed to communicate a certain resignation, like, *OK. I'm done. You got me. I'm going to die. Are you happy about it?*

Was he? Was Hunter happy about it? Forget for a moment who shot him. Was he happy to see this hunt a success, to see this beautiful animal bleed out like this? This was a huge part of the whole point of hunting. In his head he knew this was right, that if Yumi hadn't shot this deer, a wolf or cougar might have killed it, savagely. This was nature. He'd been through all the arguments a thousand times in his head, but it was different now, watching the buck in his last moments.

The buck kept looking at him. Hunter started to raise his rifle to put the deer out of his misery, but then the buck stretched his neck, his whole body shaking. His eyes went wide. Then he laid his head down on the grass, and with one final, shaking groan, the deer died.

"How do you feel?" Annette said quietly after a long moment.

"Are you going to write what I say in the newspaper?" Hunter asked.

"No," she said. "I just want to know if you're OK."

He didn't take his eyes off the deer. "I'm not a baby."

"Of course not," she said. "You're a decent human being who respects nature and doesn't like to see any living creature suffer. You're a hunter."

"I didn't shoot—"

"You might have, if Yumi had given you more time. Anyway, you tracked him, found him here." Annette twisted a lock of hair around her finger. "From what I've learned today, the point of hunting is taking an animal, not just killing it. Tracking the animal is as much a part of hunting as shooting it."

"Maybe," Hunter said, stepping up to the deer. It was a fine buck, and Yumi had shot it right where Dad, and Grandpa, and Uncle Rick always said they should. "Now we just have to figure out how to get this big guy out of here."

Hunter set about the next task, finding Yumi and Uncle Rick and maybe the others to see about bringing this deer home.

CHAPTER 13

"WHAT DO WE DO NOW?" ANNETTE ASKED HUNTER AS
they both looked down at the buck.

"I'll go back for Uncle Rick," Hunter said. "You OK to stay
here?"

"Am I OK to stand here in the woods?" Annette replied.
"Yeah, Hunter, I'm not helpless."

"Sorry," Hunter said. He was eager to get back to check on
Uncle Rick and to figure out what they were supposed to do with
this deer now. "That's not what I meant."

"It's fine," Annette said. "I was just teasing you."

Hunter took off his blaze-orange vest. "Here." He threw the
vest up on a branch overhead. "It should be safe to go without
my vest. Nobody else ought to be shooting out here. I'll be
better able to find my way back with that bright thing hanging
up there."

"But can you find your way back to Yumi and your uncle?"
Annette asked.

Hunter shrugged. "Oh yeah. I know these woods. No

problem." He did not feel as confident as he sounded, but he didn't want to admit that to Annette. He started up the slope in the direction from which they had come, stopping at the crest of the hill to look back at Annette. She smiled and waved. Hunter allowed himself a little sigh and kept going, looking for the signs he'd followed on his way to the deer.

Somehow, without the excitement of the chase, the way back seemed longer than the path on which they'd pursued the buck. Despite what Annette had said, Hunter began to worry about her. The sun was getting low, and if he was growing nervous about being alone in these woods, how must Annette feel?

Finally, Hunter caught a glimpse of blaze-orange out of the corner of his eye, and realized he was off course a little. He backtracked through some heavy tall shrubbery toward Yumi and Uncle Rick, but stopped, noticing the two of them were involved in a tense conversation.

"This is pathetic," Uncle Rick said as he rubbed his ankle. "I can't believe . . ." Grimacing in a lot of pain, he managed to stand, almost all of his weight on his good left leg. He took a tiny hobbling step and groaned.

Hunter was surprised they hadn't spotted him, but realized he'd left his blaze-orange vest in the tree back by Annette and the buck. He was blending in perfectly in all his camouflage.

Yumi reached out to her father timidly. "Can I help? Maybe I could—"

"No, I got it." Uncle Rick kept going, with little hop-limp steps. He even sped up, though nobody would really call that speed. Just a jerky, painful, limping movement, a few inches at a time. At one point, he even put the butt of his rifle to the ground and tried to use the weapon as a crutch. Was the rifle clear? If there was a round in the chamber and it accidentally went off, it could kill him.

But he was in pain, and he was mad, and he was, Hunter was pretty sure, embarrassed. Though why he should be ashamed just because he was hurt, Hunter didn't know. Yumi looked at her father worriedly.

He kept making his ridiculously slow and painful movement in the direction Hunter and Annette had gone. The sun was low in the west, and with the mountains in the distance, it would set even earlier than elsewhere.

"Dad, we're losing the light," Yumi said, free of the bitterness and whininess that she'd displayed earlier.

"I know!" Uncle Rick snapped. Sweat beaded on his face. "Do you honestly think I don't know that?" He kept inching forward. Too slow. This was never going to work.

"Dad, can I help to—"

"I said I'm fine." Uncle Rick grunted again as he tried to speed up.

Yumi closed her eyes and breathed deep as if trying to calm herself, but Hunter knew her well enough to know she couldn't edge out the anger. She watched Uncle Rick hobble a few yards past her. She folded her arms in frustration.

Hunter frowned. Why did Uncle Rick keep saying he was fine when he obviously wasn't? Why wouldn't he let Yumi help him? Hunter thought about calling out to offer help, but if Uncle Rick wouldn't accept Yumi's assistance, he wouldn't lean on Hunter. Or, worse, he *would* let Hunter help, and Yumi would be furious.

"Dad," Yumi tried again. "Maybe if you used me as a crutch, we could—"

"Yumi! I don't need your help! I don't want your help! The last thing I want is to lean on my own little girl—"

"I'm twelve! I'm not a little girl! And you do need help! You do!" Her eyes watered, and as hard as Yumi bit her lip to keep from crying, she couldn't stop the tears and quickly wiped her wet cheeks. "You act like you're fine, you say you're fine, but you're not! You've been hiding at the lodge out here in the woods for over a month! That's not fine! That's messed-up!" As her tears broke loose, a month of sorrow, anger, and frustration came gushing out.

Uncle Rick opened his mouth to speak, but he shook his head and stopped himself.

"Mom does the same thing. She acts like everything is normal. She acts like you being gone doesn't bother her, but it does. I hear her crying at night sometimes. Worse is how she acts happier than she ought to be, like it's a super-joy to make toast or clean the sink. Why doesn't anyone talk honestly about anything? Why won't you talk to me, I'm your daughter, why won't you *talk* to me?"

She sobbed, mumbled a curse. For a moment Hunter

thought she might hit her dad. Then she shook her head and sobbed again, her shoulders slumping as if she were deflating.

Now Hunter was sure he couldn't reveal himself to them. He was kind of trapped. If he emerged from his concealment, they'd know he'd been listening and Yumi would turn her wrath on him.

"Yumi . . ." Uncle Rick reached out a shaky hand. "Can we . . . can we talk about this later?"

"When? That's all you and Mom ever say. We'll talk about this later, Yumi. Not now, Yumi. This isn't a good time, Yumi." She kicked a rock and sent it skittering a few feet. "When? When will we finally try to fix this?"

"I don't . . ." Uncle Rick slapped his fist on his chest and blinked watery eyes. "I don't know if I can be fixed, kid. I think maybe I'm broken. I've been home from the war for years, but still sometimes I . . ." He slung his rifle and ran his hands down over his face. "I can't stop thinking about it! I want it out of my head, but I can't get it out of my head, it won't stop, it won't stop!" He sniffled and shook his head. "This isn't the kind of thing for a kid to hear—"

"Dad, *tell* me. *Please.* I just shot a deer. I'm not a baby."

"You don't get it. I didn't want all the . . . from over there, coming back to you."

"I want to know about what happened over there. I've read online all about 9/11 and the Afghanistan war. But I know next to nothing about what you did over there. Dad, you earned a

Bronze Star. A bunch of other medals. Why won't you tell me about that? You're a hero."

"No!" He threw his rifle to the ground, an unthinkable act. Hunter had heard of rifles going off from less than that. Yumi would have been grounded until she was sixteen for doing that.

"I'm no stupid hero! Me and my guys got lit up! That's all! I should have ordered my squad to take a different route. Our convoys had driven through that intersection way too many times. And every time it had been fine. There was another way we could have gone to get to this meeting at the governor's compound but we were running late. So, I said we'd take the short way. The usual way." His face was red. Tears ran down his cheeks. "The *usual* way! If we know the usual way, so does the enemy. And they did. And I should have known something was wrong because that intersection is usually packed with chaos traffic, and that morning it was wide-open. Basically nobody else there. And the Taliban ripped into us from on top of the buildings from all directions."

Hunter watched his uncle, the brave hero, the man who had literally been through a minefield. And now his armor of strength and courage and always knowing what to do was cracked, and beneath it was this man who was so sad and so afraid.

"People have called me a hero. I *hate* that. I was just an idiot. Criminally negligent. Because our lead Humvee was disabled and my troopers were being shot up. So I threw one grenade on one roof and a second on another, and rushed up to get my guys out of there so we could withdraw." He wiped his nose. "We lost two guys. Another hurt real bad, still has problems. And I wake up from nightmares about the whole thing. And I can't stop thinking about it, and sometimes I get so . . ."—he gritted his teeth and squeezed his hands into shaking fists—"so angry about it. And I . . . and I . . . I didn't want all that ugliness . . . polluting my family's life."

"But we miss you so much," Yumi said. "You could never pollute my life. You're my daddy."

Her dad sobbed, and almost dropped, so that Yumi rushed to his side. Without saying a word, she picked up his rifle for him, and she grabbed his hand and put his arm around her shoulders.

"I'm so sorry," Uncle Rick said.

"It's OK. We're OK. Or we will be." They were quiet for a moment. "Let's just go get that deer," Yumi said. "Lean on me."

"Are you sure you—" But Uncle Rick took a step, testing her out as a crutch, and she braced herself against the weight he put on her. She smiled, despite the obvious strain, as though happy her father felt he could depend on her. And together the two of them made their way up the hill and on toward the deer they'd worked together to bring down.

Hunter was about to show himself when Yumi spoke up. A part of him felt terrible for accidentally eavesdropping on the moment, but he somehow also understood the two of them needed this conversation. Hunter didn't know too much about this kind of stuff, but even he understood that whatever tension had been building between these two needed to be released.

"You said you were sorry," Yumi said softly, but loud enough for her father and Hunter to hear. "I should apologize too. You got shot at, got shot, and I act like you staying at the lodge is so tough."

"No, Yumi," her dad said. "Don't apologize for feeling bad. It's my job to be there for you, and I haven't been doing my job."

Yumi opened her mouth to speak, but stopped herself, frowning and biting her lip. Finally she tried again. "I only mean I haven't been making this any easier for you. I'm sorry about that. Even just this hunting trip. I kind of acted like a spoiled brat, complaining when you wanted me to come along."

Uncle Rick stepped on an uneven rock and groaned, speaking really fast through the pain. "No, it was great because I had the chance to meet your friend Annette." He let out a long breath. "She's pretty cool. Almost as cool as you, kid."

Hunter let the two of them walk well past him before he started following. "Uncle Rick? Yumi?" he called out after a moment. They stopped, and he hurried to catch up with them. "I got all turned around coming back to find you. Just spotted your blaze-orange a second ago. We found the buck! Come on! I'll show you the way!"

"Good job, Higgins," Yumi said.

"You need any help, Uncle Rick?" Hunter asked.

Uncle Rick smiled and looked at his daughter. "I got all the help I need."

Hunter led them back through the woods until he finally spotted his blaze-orange vest hanging in the branch. "There!"

As the three of them approached Annette and the buck, Yumi looked up and met her dad's smile with one of her own.

"He's big, ain't he?" Uncle Rick said.

"He's incredible," Yumi said.

"Feeling any better, Uncle Rick?" Hunter said.

"Ankle still hurts like crazy." He squeezed Yumi's shoulder. "But I feel better than I've been in a long time. Not one hundred percent, but getting better."

"Come on!" Annette took out her phone. "We need to get a photo while we still have the light! I've seen posts online. If you kill a deer, you're supposed to lift its head up and pose for a photo."

Yumi checked with her father. He leaned his rifle against a nearby fallen tree trunk and rested against the mossy wood himself. "She's right," he said. "Go on. I'm good here."

With some reluctance, Yumi left her father's side and hurried to the deer. She knelt behind it and, taking hold of its antlers, lifted the head upright, smiling over her first deer.

Hunter tried his best to appear happy for his cousin, to keep any trace of bitterness or disappointment from his expression as Annette took pictures, but Yumi must have seen through him.

"Come on, Higgins. You tracked this big guy. Get in here for a photo."

"Seriously?" Hunter asked.

"Yeah. Hurry up!" Yumi said.

Hunter felt a little weird, like he was hogging the credit for the kill, but maybe it was OK. He had tracked the buck after he was hit. It had been a team effort taking the deer. It certainly would take a group effort to haul the big thing back to the lodge.

"Why don't all three of you kids get in this photo?" Uncle Rick said after Annette had photographed Yumi and Hunter. He eased himself off the log and slowly made his way to Annette, holding out his hand for her phone.

Annette looked at Yumi and Hunter as if to ask if it was OK if she joined them. Yumi laughed. "Get in here, Annette!"

She rushed to them, dropping to her knees on Yumi's left. Hunter pressed in on Yumi's right. All three of them smiled from behind the buck's rack.

"OK. I want to make sure I take my time with this. Don't want to waste the film," Uncle Rick said.

"The what?" Hunter asked.

"He's making a terrible joke like her phone is an old-fashioned camera from the 1900s," Yumi explained.

"Ah." Hunter forced a little laugh. "Good one."

Uncle Rick laughed for real, returning Annette's phone. He whipped out his antler-handled Buck knife and flipped open its four-inch blade. "Now we need to get this deer skinned, field-dressed, and quartered, while he's still warm. This is the part where it gets pretty bloody."

CHAPTER 14

"IT'S GETTING DARK," SAID UNCLE RICK. "SO INSTEAD OF talking you through and having you do this, I'm going to show you how to field-dress this deer." He held up the knife. "Had this Buck knife since I was sixteen. You gotta have a good knife. Sharp and sturdy. Use a small knife? It's no good. A little blade could turn in your hand when it hits bone. You'll wind up slicing your fingers off." He pointed at the deer. "Help me get the animal on his back, pull the head uphill."

Hunter grabbed the buck by the neck and pulled, grunting. "He's heavy."

"Yeah, he is." Uncle Rick laughed. "Put your back into it!"

Annette looked as reluctant to grab hold of the dead animal as Hunter had felt, but she bit her lip and wrapped her arms around it, helping Hunter pull the head up the slope.

"Hold up a sec," Yumi said, running over to the big log and leaning her rifle against the wood next to her dad's gun. "Just wait, you guys!" She rushed back and pushed against the deer's front shoulder, not seeming to care at all as blood seeped from its wound between her fingers. "Come on! Let's *move* this thing."

The deer slid in the grass so his head was uphill, and the three of them, with some help from Uncle Rick, rolled him onto his back.

"That's the way. Put rocks under his shoulders. Help keep him from rolling." Uncle Rick slid rocks beneath the buck's hips. With practiced efficiency, he sliced around and under the buck's genitals. "Don't want urine and all that on the meat," he explained.

Annette held up her phone. "Now that the hunt is over, would it be OK if I got some video?"

Uncle Rick nodded. "If you think there's enough light. Go ahead." He slipped the tip of his blade into the deer between his hind legs. "We want to slit the skin and peel it back before cutting through the muscle layer. This will help keep hair away from the meat. Plus"—he cut and peeled back skin—"it will make it easier to see what we're doing. So I'm gonna make this shallow slit all the way to the breastbone up close to the head." He was quiet for a moment as he worked. "What do you think, Yumi? You want this head mounted? Your first kill on the wall of the lodge?"

Hunter looked away. For the rest of his life, this deer's head would be a monument, a reminder of how he had not been able to summon the will to kill and Yumi had. Yumi was cool about it, yeah, talking about how he'd done a good job tracking the animal, bringing him and Annette in on the photo. But on the drive home, there would be no congratulations from Dad about the great buck he'd brought down. When Mom asked how the hunt went, he could only tell her about failure and wait for another at-least-you-got-fourth speech.

"Yeah," Yumi said. "I think he's definitely a trophy."

"In that case"—Uncle Rick kept cutting—"we cut only to the breastbone, here behind the forelegs." He turned the blade upward, holding it in a sort of reverse grip, trailing it with his left hand. "Now through the muscle, spreading everything open as we go."

Steam rose from the incision, and Uncle Rick's hands were covered in the warm red blood that soaked the grass where the buck had died. Still he cut, quickly but carefully, his muscles straining as he sawed through the breastbone cartilage. He explained cutting to remove the anus as well as slicing through the windpipe and esophagus.

Hunter thought he heard something, a rustling of leaves. Was that a twig snapping? He turned to scan the shadowy woods, but saw nothing.

"Now the really gross part," Uncle Rick said. Hunter turned his attention back to the matter at hand as his uncle gripped the bloody hose of the windpipe. "I gotta pull this real hard and . . ." A whole mess of organs slid down to the deer's midsection. Hunter wrinkled his nose, watching, trying to ignore the squishing and sucking sounds as it all moved around.

"How do you know how to do all this?" Annette said, circling around to get a better video angle. "You're like a surgeon."

"Well, I'm not cutting for the first time." Uncle Rick smiled. "Years of practice. My dad first showed me how to do this when I was about your age. He kept teaching me with every deer we took. So I'd end up doing this a couple of times every year. There really aren't that many steps. Just have to be willing to get your hands dirty, try not to think about how gross it is. It's just meat prep."

Hunter noticed Annette frowning, looking into the distance up the sharp slope behind him.

"What is it?" Hunter asked, turning to see whatever she'd noticed. There was nothing.

"Thought I saw something move up there, behind that clump of trees." Annette shrugged. "Just for a moment. Must be a trick of the light."

"Twilight can be weird like that," said Uncle Rick. "The changing light. The spreading shadows. It can fool us. Look like movement." He returned his attention to the deer. "Now we turn him on his side."

Yumi and Hunter rushed to remove the rocks and help turn the deer. Uncle Rick cut around the ribs, then had them turn the buck over to cut tissue away from the other set of ribs.

"Here we go," said Uncle Rick. "Fun time."

A bloody gooey mess of entrails pulled out of the animal in one squelchy movement. "When we do this, we want to try to keep any gut juices away from the meat as much as we can."

"OK, now, that's gross." Annette pressed the back of her hand over her mouth and nose.

Uncle Rick laughed. "Yeah. Just focus on how good the meat will taste."

Yumi laughed too. "I kind of don't want to think about eating at all right now."

Annette glanced back at the woods for a moment, then pointed at the entrails. "I'm sorry to be the baby here. I've cleaned fish before, but the largest fish I've ever caught is half the size of all that muck."

"There's more to do," said Uncle Rick. "Can you all try to find some clean, straight sticks? About a foot long? We'll need them to prop the buck open to cool him down. Yumi, when I lift him up by his hind legs, you slide that big rock under his rump. We gotta cut through his pelvis."

Hunter and Annette went looking for sticks. Spotting a possibly suitable candidate, if the thin limb was snapped in half, Hunter shifted his slung rifle from his shoulder onto his back. Holding the wood over his knee, he pulled until it snapped loudly.

Then there was a second snap.

Hunter looked to Annette who was still searching for a stick.

Uncle Rick and Yumi had stopped working and, on their knees next to the deer, straightened up, listening.

Annette saw it first. She gasped and almost dropped her phone.

A low, mean growl added to the chill in the valley.

Up on the hill, standing in the space between two towering pines, was a massive gray wolf. He bared his rows of sharp white teeth, long top and bottom fangs like daggers.

"Daddy?" Yumi's voice shook.

"Oh no," said Uncle Rick.

Annette moved closer to Hunter.

The wolf raised his head toward the first stars in the sky, and its deep ghostly howl echoed through the woods. He took a few steps closer, muscles taut and ready. The wolf had other plans for Yumi's deer.

CHAPTER 15

THE WOLF'S HARD MUSCLE WAS CLEARLY VISIBLE EVEN under all his fur. If he stood erect he would be as big as a man. His head was larger than Hunter's, with huge jaws that instantly conveyed power. The beast could probably bite clean through someone's whole neck, gnawing a person's head off. His paws were as large as Hunter's fists, with sharp black claws visible even from thirty yards away.

Hunter had never seen a wolf in real life. He'd seen photos and videos of them online. They were featured on the local news. People around McCall talked about them. But this wasn't some far-off news story or one of their hunting videos. This was real, right there, right now. The creature was hungry.

The wolf glared at them with one golden eye. His left eye and ear were gone, replaced by a nasty jagged scar that left his lip permanently curled into a fearsome snarl.

"Everybody stay still," Uncle Rick said quietly.

He needn't have said so. All four of them froze instinctively, an action born of some old memory of someone's angry pet dog.

But this was no dog. The wolf wanted that deer, and Hunter figured he didn't care who he had to hurt to get it.

Uncle Rick looked at his rifle, next to Yumi's, leaning against the fallen tree trunk, twenty yards away. "I'm gonna go for my weapon. As soon as I move, you kids run, fast as you can, back toward the lodge. Don't stop for anything."

"Dad. No way." Yumi's voice was shaky. "We're not leaving you."

"Don't argue with me." Uncle Rick was like a different person. Efficient. Cold. The wolf, hearing Uncle Rick's tone, growled again. Uncle Rick looked at Yumi, Annette, and Hunter in turn. "You do what I say. When I say go, you run fast as you can. Hopefully the wolf will go for the deer first. I'll get to my gun."

"You're hurt," Yumi said. "You'll be too slow. You'll never make it."

"Yumi, don't argue with—"

The wolf lunged. He flew forward a full body length. His legs touched down and shoved him forward even faster. For such a big creature, he moved, he raced, he flew forward with blur-fast speed. Teeth bared, rage in his eye. Annette screamed. Uncle Rick cursed.

Hunter sprinted forward, slammed-cranked his rifle's bolt action. He raised his weapon as he halted, squared up his feet, and fired.

The wolf yelped as blood burst from his chest above his leg. He howled. He roared. But after only a minor stumble he kept rushing forward, ten yards from the deer, Uncle Rick, and Yumi. Hunter cranked his rifle's bolt handle up, backward, forward, down—and shot again.

The wolf's eye went wide. He let loose a loud long screech of a yelp. He dropped to the ground, his great head skidding along for a foot on a bed of pine needles.

Hunter didn't wait a moment, but ejected his spent casing and chambered another round. He kept his rifle stock to his cheek. If the wolf made another move, Hunter would shoot him in the head. He wouldn't miss from this range.

Only then, with a moment to think about what had happened in the last few seconds, did Hunter realize what he had done. One moment the deadly animal had been about to attack his family. The next it was down.

Hunter hadn't thought about the beauty of the wolf, hadn't considered for a second whether or not he was capable of killing him. Killing the wolf wasn't even his goal. Not really. All he'd cared about was protecting his family and Annette. Killing the wolf was only a means toward that end.

The wolf met his gaze, and Hunter understood the beast. He felt the sort of connection with his prey that his father had described back at the lodge. The wolf groaned, blood spilling on the ground before him.

Hunter had watched too many movies where the bad guy or the monster, thought dead, suddenly sprang up, out of desperation or revenge, for one last surprise attack. He would not let his guard down now. He kept his rifle aimed at the wolf, slowly moving closer, the better to score a final lethal shot if he needed to do so.

But eventually Hunter knew it wouldn't come to that. The fight had gone out of the animal. The wolf watched him approach. He had stopped growling, stopped snarling now. He labored to draw raspy breaths.

Hunter looked the wolf in his eye. The wolf wasn't evil. He didn't hate them. He didn't hate Hunter even as his death approached. The wolf was hungry. He was part of nature. And survival in nature, survival anywhere, depended on feeding.

There was a sharp beauty in the wolf's lethal ferocity. Hunter knew that, even as he'd been forced to end it. "I'm sorry," he said quietly to the wolf. "I had no choice."

The wolf huffed, watching him. Then he shook, legs jerking, and, lifting his head, he opened his jaws, showing his lethal teeth and letting loose one final, bone-chilling howl.

The wolf breathed his last, and lay dead at Hunter's feet.

For a long, long moment, all four of them watched the dead animal where it rested. Nobody spoke. Nobody moved.

As Hunter's pounding heart and fast breathing began to calm, he wondered, even with the evidence right there in front of him, if he had truly killed the wolf. He felt as he sometimes did in the first few minutes after waking from a dream, not quite sure where he was or what had really just happened.

"Well," Annette said. Her voice made Hunter jump, and he took that opportunity to finally lower his rifle and click its safety back on so that he didn't accidentally shoot someone. Annette approached and gently patted his shoulder. "Looks like you are a hunter after all."

That broke the spell of silence.

Yumi burst out, "Higgins, you just shot a wolf!"

Uncle Rick sat down and leaned back, his blood-soaked hands on the ground behind him. He looked up and blew out a long breath. The wolf had fallen about five yards from him. "I haven't had a close call like that since Afghanistan."

Yumi fell to her knees beside her father and put her arms around him, leaning her head on his shoulder. Slowly, still quite stunned, Uncle Rick sat up and put his arm around his daughter.

"Hey, Uncle Rick," Hunter said.

It took his uncle a moment to respond. "Yeah, buddy?"

"I don't have a license or tags to hunt wolf. Am I in trouble?"

Uncle Rick laughed, and then they all laughed, as if the dam had just broken on their stunned tension.

"Do you mean in more trouble than being attacked by a huge wolf?" Yumi asked.

"Hey!" Hunter smiled. "There are laws. Poaching is a serious crime."

"Hunter," said Uncle Rick, "you have every right to self-defense. We'll have to explain what happened to the game warden, but he'll understand. No hunter is required to let an animal attack him or his family just because the animal's out of season or he has no permit."

Hunter frowned. "But how will they know that the wolf—"

"Because I have the most amazing video of the whole thing."

Annette held up her phone, the image of the wolf paused in the video on-screen. "Started filming the field dressing of the deer and was still recording when the wolf showed up. I have video of the whole event. That should be enough proof it was self defense, right?"

Uncle Rick nodded. "More than enough. And I have never been so glad about anyone having a phone out here."

"So, Uncle Rick, do you think we could take this wolf to the taxidermist too?" Hunter said. "I think he'd make a pretty good trophy."

CHAPTER 16

"HUNTER!" DAD'S VOICE ECHOED FROM THE DARK WOODS.

"Rick?" Grandpa called a moment later.

"Over here!" Yumi shouted.

"We heard the howl," Dad said. "Heard the shots. Is there a wolf out here? Did you see—" He spotted the wolf carcass on the ground. "Oh wow!"

"Hunter's not afraid of the big bad wolf," Annette said.

Grandpa looked, open-mouthed, at the wolf. "You, Hunter?"

"It was attacking. Higgins totally saved us." Yumi told Grandpa and Dad the whole story, from her shooting the deer, to Hunter and Annette tracking it, to the wolf's deadly charge and Hunter's two shots.

"Sorry," Hunter said, remembering what he'd always been taught about hunting. "I didn't check to make sure I had a clear shot and everything. I guess I didn't think."

"No, you just saved everyone's lives," Grandpa said. "You seized the moment when it really counted. Great job, Hunter."

Dad wrapped Hunter up in a firm one-armed side hug. "I knew you were a hunter, son. I just had no idea you'd be this great."

"Two great new hunters in the family!" Grandpa boomed. "Let's get these animals back to the lodge so we can celebrate a successful first hunt!"

With everybody all together, they might have been able to carry the buck out all at once, but since they wanted the wolf intact, to stuff the whole thing, like Reagan the bear, they would have to make more than one trip. They had to quarter the deer, dividing it into five parts, four parts to be broken down for food, plus his head. The parts they could not carry on the first trip, they would hang from trees by the ropes they carried, so that no more hungry wolves or other animals could steal their prize. Dad and Grandpa gutted and drained the wolf, not for the sake of its meat, but to make it lighter for the two of them to carry back to the lodge. Yumi managed one quarter of the deer, Hunter another, and Annette a third. Uncle Rick's ankle was feeling a little better, but still bothered him, so that he would come back for the last part of the deer when his ankle could better handle the load.

On such a long walk, through what was basically full-on darkness, carrying his rifle and his part of the deer became quite a challenge, though Hunter suspected it was nothing compared to what Grandpa and Dad were suffering lugging that wolf through the woods. It didn't take long before the happy chatter they'd enjoyed when they first set out fell to silence and the occasional laborious grunt.

Grandpa eventually managed to find cell service on the walk and called the game warden, who was waiting at the lodge when everyone returned.

Hunter was nervous when he saw the man's shiny badge and his gun, but his first question was, "Is anyone hurt? Does anyone require medical attention?"

Uncle Rick laughed. "I'm hurt, but not because of the wolf." He explained about his ankle.

"Lone wolf, huh? Rare, but it happens." The officer focused on Hunter. "You shot this wolf in self-defense?"

Hunter explained the incident, and Annette showed the video. It was the first time Hunter had seen it. Although in his head he knew it had happened, in his heart it still felt fake, like he was watching someone else.

"Wow, son," said the officer. "You look like some kind of action hero, rushing in there to save everybody like that. Great shooting."

"My cousin's the best shooter in the county!" Yumi said.

The officer hooked his fingers in his equipment belt and laughed a little. "That so? That's really saying something, there, miss. This is Idaho, after all. Got a lot of fine shooters here. The state is even shaped like a gun!"

The men all laughed. Hunter forced himself to appear amused as well, though he was still worried about being in trouble for killing the wolf.

"Well, even without the video, all of these witnesses are proof enough that this was self-defense. I have a few forms for you to fill out, just so I have an official statement for the record. You can mail it in. Meantime, I'm just happy everybody's OK."

The officer handed Dad the paperwork, swung up into his pickup, and drove away.

After that, it was time to go back to retrieve the last of the deer. Annette asked why they didn't just leave it for crows. Didn't they have enough? Grandpa explained that they never wasted the animals they took.

Uncle Rick offered to go with Hunter to get the last of the meat. Grandpa and Dad tried to argue, but he insisted he was feeling better, with just a bit of a limp left. There was an awkward moment as the three men exchanged a meaningful look, before everyone agreed.

No longer worried about scaring off animals they were trying to hunt, Uncle Rick and Hunter were equipped with bright LED headlamps and 3200-lumen LED flashlights. They also carried their rifles. Hunting was illegal at night, and a passing Idaho Fish and Game officer might ask questions, but after the wolf, neither of them were going out into the night unarmed.

"You're walking a lot better," Hunter said after a long silence. They'd been moving slowly to accommodate for Uncle Rick's remaining limp.

"It doesn't hurt so bad now."

They continued on the path back to where they'd hung up the last of the deer, navigating by following footprints, blood, and landmarks they remembered.

"I always thought that the trip back out to retrieve the meat we couldn't at first carry is the longest trip of them all. It feels like the remains of the deer move farther away when we're not paying attention."

"Like a zombie?" Hunter asked.

Uncle Rick chuckled. "Yeah, I guess. I wish there was a better way to bring the animals in."

"Do you always do it this way?" Hunter asked.

"No. Sometimes the terrain is even and clear enough for someone to drive out with the four-wheeler, and we can load the entire deer to take it back in one trip. Sometimes the deer is small enough for a couple men to carry at once. But whenever it's big enough that we have to quarter the animal, it just takes forever. I've hunted alone. Brought down a huge moose once way out there. I had to take separate trips for each of the four big pieces. I must have walked about thirty miles that day. Was tired after that. Bone-tired. Army-tired."

A while later, they reached the site where Uncle Rick had dressed the deer. Three coyotes were digging into the entrails, blood soaking their faces and paws. They were interested in the quarter carcass the family had hung from the tree.

"Go on! Get out of here!" Uncle Rick shouted. The coyotes scattered. "Worthless things." Uncle Rick untied the rope, taking hold of the last part of the buck. "All right. Final trip of the night."

"You sure you got it?" Hunter had to ask. Uncle Rick was still hurting.

"Yeah. No problem."

They walked back through the cold dark in silence. Once a raccoon scurried away from the light. They heard other movements in the dark woods around them. Hunter tried not to think about the possibility of more wolves, or a cougar, out here. The Idaho wilderness was real, not always safe, and it was not for the timid or fearful. It required a certain amount of courage. He understood that now.

"Hunter, you saved my life. More importantly, you saved my daughter's life." Most of the time when Uncle Rick talked to him, there was a playfulness, a kind of jokey tone in his voice. He usually sounded the same as he did when he said stuff like, "Hey buddy! What's the sitrep?" or "How's my favorite nephew rocking the sixth grade?" But tonight as they walked, all the jokes and humor were washed away. The man sounded even more serious, somehow, than he had when the two of them had talked about killing and war.

"I've been around the world. I've been through the desert with guns, stopping highway robbers and other bad guys, riding into town to try to help the good people. A lot of it was horrible, and I wanted to come home the whole time. But it was also an adventure. Still, nothing compared to the adventure of growing up."

Hunter looked warily at his uncle for a moment. Was this going to be one of those I-miss-the-good-old-days speeches his father had started giving him lately?

Uncle Rick must have sensed his wariness, because he laughed and held up his free hand. "Just hang in there and listen a minute. Try not to shrug off everything I'm saying just because I'm old."

"You're not old."

"Because I'm *starting* to get old. OK? You're twelve. There will be so many more friends, so many fun times with them. Sports. Parties. Dates."

"Oh no, is this, like, The Talk?" Hunter joked.

"No!" Uncle Rick's shout echoed through the woods. A coyote howled somewhere. "That's absolutely in no way *my* job!" His fun tone was back. "And there will be a bunch more outdoor fun, more hunting and fishing and hiking for you. And because of you, all those things lie ahead for my daughter too." His voice shook a little as he said the last part. "There were men in the war with me to whom I owe my life, and they're like brothers to me, and I'll always be grateful to them. But, Hunter . . . none of them saved my Yumi. Do you get what I'm trying to say?"

"You don't have to thank me or anything. I killed that wolf as much to save myself. Not even that. I didn't even—"

"Didn't even think about it?"

Hunter was confused for a moment. But of course Uncle Rick knew just what he was talking about. "Yeah. I barely remember it. I certainly didn't think anything like, *Oh no. I have to save my family.*"

"Exactly." Uncle Rick stopped walking and turned to face Hunter, looking at him with tears in his eyes. "So it's pretty tough when people call you a hero, huh?"

They were silent for a while. Finally they both nodded and kept walking.

"What I'm about to tell you is hard to explain. I have a brother, your dad. But the guys with whom I served in that war are my *brother* brothers. You get me? I mean, I love your dad. Of course. But there's a different connection with someone who's saved your life, and especially with someone who's saved the life of your kid. Which you won't entirely understand for many years because you're not a father."

"I don't know what to say," Hunter confessed.

"Oh, that's OK!" Uncle Rick laughed. "I said this bond is hard to explain, and I think that's one of the many reasons why none of us ever really talks about it. I just want to say, this once, thank you for saving us. And I think, without us saying much more about it, you and I have an understanding and connection now."

"And Yumi and Annette?" He'd spoken without thinking and almost immediately wished he hadn't.

"Well, Yumi's your cousin and friend for life. I've always been happy to see the two of you hanging out. Now, Annette, on the other hand. Come on, I could tell you weren't too excited when she first showed up. But now you totally saved her life. So, you know . . ."

"Please stop." Hunter laughed.

"What!" Uncle Rick laughed too. "I'm just saying maybe you can ask her to couple-skate at the next skating party!"

"Are you kidding?" Hunter fired back. He was glad it was so

dark. His cheeks must be flaming red. "Nobody couple-skates. I don't even know what that is."

"Fair enough. But she is pretty cool, right?" said Uncle Rick.

"She's OK," said Hunter.

"All right. Listen. Seriously," Uncle Rick said. "And I'll say this just one more time, and then let it drop. Hunter. Thank you for saving Yumi and me. I'll never forget it."

CHAPTER 17

"THERE HE IS!" GRANDPA SHOUTED WHEN HUNTER entered the lodge. "Sureshot Higgins, the wolf slayer!"

Hunter laughed. Everybody had showered and changed clothes. There were big bowls of popcorn and nachos loaded with cheese, venison, olives, and a pile of other great stuff. Grandpa had already cracked his second beer. The girls were drinking sodas, sitting by the fire again.

"Hey, I wouldn't even have shot the thing if we hadn't needed to defend Yumi's deer," Hunter said.

"For which, thank you very much!" Yumi raised her drink in salute.

"Where's my dad?" Hunter asked.

"Out in the butcher shop," said Grandpa. "I expect he's about done skinning your wolf. Sorry. He didn't want to wait. It's harder to remove the skin the more the animal cools off. Then he's going to go ahead and butcher the deer. Yumi says deer steaks tonight. You hungry?"

"Sounds great!" Hunter said.

"Higgins!" Yumi shouted. "Would you get cleaned up already? We're going out to the Tower."

"I should probably go help my dad," Hunter said.

"Hunter," Grandpa said. "It's fine. It's really not much of a two-person job. You've done enough. Take it easy."

Hunter shrugged and went out to the shop area to ditch his dirty cold-weather gear before heading in to shower and then putting on a clean McCall Warriors sweatshirt and jeans. Minutes later, grabbing his regular coat, hat, and a pair of gloves, he went with Yumi and Annette out into the dark. Annette carried the flashlight. Yumi had a heavy blanket, a box of hand warmers, and a bag of her favorite snack, pretzels. Hunter carried a small cooler packed with cans of soda.

"Tell me again why we have to be out here in the cold?" Hunter asked.

"Higgins! It's simple." Yumi reached the base of the Tower first. "Hanging out with adults is no good. We can't talk around them. They barge into every conversation, to either correct you or to tell you that whatever you're talking about reminds them of how it was thirty years ago or something. Fine. The nineties were great. Whatever! I don't need to hear about it."

Yumi climbed up the crevice to the top of the Tower. She turned and reached down as Hunter handed up the blanket and then the cooler. Soon all three of them sat on the blanket enjoying pretzels and drinks.

"You guys," Annette said, "this is going to be the best story the *McCall Middle School Times* has ever published. A hunting story. A wolf attack. A freaking *wolf*!"

"No joke, that was terrifying," Yumi said.

"Plus the video I got can be posted to the online edition," Annette added. "How's that possibly not going to go viral?"

"Oh yeah, a million views," Yumi said. "You'll be one of those YouTube stars. Next you'll be getting sponsors, demonstrating nail polish or whatever."

The girls laughed. "I haven't worn nail polish since I was like five or something."

"Seriously?" Yumi opened a can of soda, took a long drink, and let go a little burp.

Annette grabbed a handful of pretzels from the bag. "I just don't see the point. Why would I want different-colored fingernails or toenails? Seriously, Hunter, do guys like that? Do all the boys hang out talking about the color of a girl's fingernails?"

Hunter didn't hang around a lot of the guys that much. He spent more time with Yumi than with anyone else. But for some reason, in the face of Annette's question, and with Annette sitting next to him, he didn't want to admit to that.

"The guys mostly talk about sports. Which is the best team. Who's going to start in the game."

"All things you know nothing about." Yumi said it as a joke, but Hunter wasn't laughing.

"I do too know about sports," Hunter said. "I just don't care about them as much."

"Even hunting?" Annette asked.

"Hunting is a different type of sport," Yumi said. "It's more real than all that our-team-is-better-than-your-team crap. And the guys do too hang out talking about girls, I bet. Just not about their fingernails."

The girls laughed again. Hunter eventually did too. "Yeah, that's kind of true."

Yumi grabbed Annette's hand and held it out. "Do you think her fingernails are so hot, Higgins?"

Annette snatched her hand back. "Yumi!"

But Hunter knew, or sort of knew, how to play this game. "Oh yeah," he said. "Super-hot."

"Speeeeaking of fingernails," Annette said. "The claws on that wolf! That thing could have ripped our faces off."

"Yeah, but I think wolves bite more than scratch, so it almost ate our faces off," Yumi said.

"Seriously, Hunter," said Annette in her reporter voice. She pulled out her notebook and held it close to her face to try to see. She shrugged, giving up. "What were you thinking when that wolf charged? Sorry, but I about peed my pants." Everybody laughed. "But you just blasted the thing. What was going through your mind at that point?"

Hunter thought for a minute about how to answer that question.

Yumi burped, laughed, and blurted out, "He was thinking, *Oh no! I must protect my darling Annette!*"

"Yumi!" Annette and Hunter shouted together.

Yumi rolled onto her back laughing.

"I'm trying to get a good quote to help me wrap up the article," Annette said. "How did you feel when the wolf attacked? What did you think?"

"Sorry," Hunter said. He really was sorry to have to disappoint Annette on this. "But the answer to both questions is . . . nothing. There was no time. I had a gun. Nobody else did. It was the wolf or us. No contest."

"That was perfect," Annette said. She grabbed a flashlight and started writing. A moment later, she clicked her pen and put away her journalism kit. She put her hand on Hunter's forearm, and even through her gloves and his coat, it was electric. "Thank you, Hunter. For the quote, sure. But seriously, thanks for saving us."

Hunter ignored Yumi's huge smile, the snarky look on her face, the way her eyes darted from Annette to her hand to Hunter and back again.

Hunter had no idea what to say to that. In the end, he spoke the first truth that came to mind. "I'm glad you came here with us."

EVERYONE WENT OUT AGAIN VERY EARLY SUNDAY morning. Grandpa could have taken a shot at a buck, but it was only a three-by-three. He let it go. Other than that, there wasn't a lot of action going, but, although failing to find much worth shooting was never something a hunter mourned very deeply, they felt even less disappointment than they usually did. After the already legendary hunt of the day before, everyone's spirits were still flying high.

And when they came back into the lodge, the party was over. It was time to pack up to leave. Grandpa was wiping down the kitchen, an obsession of his, to avoid drawing ants or mice. Dad was taking it easy in Grandpa's recliner. Uncle Rick had been back in his bedroom for a while.

"I'm used to the Sunday night blues," Yumi said as she dropped her packed duffel bag next to the door, ready to go. She took a seat on the stool next to where Annette sat at the kitchen island counter. "When the weekend is just about over and you have to start thinking about school the next day—"

"Like, is your homework done, and do you have your books ready to go?" Annette said.

"Ugh, stop talking about it." Hunter plopped down on the third stool and put his hands over his ears.

"But today's even worse," Yumi continued.

Hunter smiled at her. He understood what she meant. He was sad this was over. It felt like they'd only just arrived.

"EOHDS," Dad said.

"What?" Hunter asked.

"End of Hunting Depression Syndrome," Dad said. "It's an epidemic. You come out here, come truly alive, live the adventure. Then . . . back to work, or school, or something that's certainly not as fun as hunting."

"I wasn't even really hunting and I think I'm suffering from the condition," Annette said.

Uncle Rick came down the hall from his bedroom, walking just fine now, two massive duffel bags slung from his left shoulder, a third hanging from his right.

"You ready to go home, Yumi?"

Yumi's face lit up with a big smile. "Yeah! Are you, um—"

"Eh, I'm tired of being out here," said Uncle Rick. "Gets kind of lonely."

"That's great!" Yumi suddenly pushed back her stool and hurried to her bag. "Just want to check to make sure I have . . ." She shuffled through her things, looking very busy, but Hunter thought he saw her wipe her eyes as she smiled.

ON THE DRIVE HOME HUNTER SAT BACK, RELAXING IN THE truck, seat reclined and seat heaters warming his bottom and back, while Dad's old music played on the truck stereo. Hunter was sure he had changed somehow, during the course of this hunting experience, but one thing about him was absolutely the same. He still wasn't a fan of the ancient songs his dad liked. He was grateful when Dad turned the stereo down.

"I'm proud of you. Your first hunt wasn't easy for you, but you didn't give up. You stuck with it, and you came through when it really counted. You really manned up out there. Good job."

"If you're so proud of me, can we listen to music that's not from the 1900s?"

Dad laughed and tapped his screen to pull up something more modern.

"How long do you think it will take the taxidermist to have my wolf ready?" Hunter asked.

"Oh, the man's busy. Tanning a lot of hides. Preparing tons of deer head mounts and other trophies. I'd say ... about eight months. Sometime this summer."

Hunter sighed. In middle school, eight months was a lifetime away. "It'll be pretty cool. You think he can preserve the scar, make it look like the way it was?"

"Our guy is the best taxidermist in the business. Your wolf will look great. And, think, every time you look at it, or if someone new comes over and asks about it, someone will tell the story of how you brought it down."

"But before that ..." Hunter said. "Before Yumi shot that deer, I couldn't ..."

"That doesn't matter," Dad said. "When people tell the story of that wolf, nobody will care if you were reluctant to shoot earlier in the day. All they'll care about is the vicious wolf. All they'll say is stuff like, *Whoa! You killed a wolf? You stopped a wolf attack?* And that's pretty cool."

Hunter said nothing, but smiled broadly. It was most certainly *not* an at-least-you-got-fourth speech.

TAPTAPTAP. HUNTER FELT THE FAMILIAR ANNOYING summons on his shoulder. He glanced at Miss Foudy, who was reading something on her computer at her desk.

TapTapTap. "Hey, Higgins," Kelton Fielding whispered. TapTapTap. "Higgins."

Hunter leaned back in his seat. "What?"

"You bag a deer?"

Miss Foudy still hadn't noticed them.

Hunter shook his head. He heard Kelton chuckle.

"Toldja you wouldn't bag no deer," Kelton whispered. "I was just about to shoot a huge buck. Eight-by-eight, at least. But Fish and Game showed up, busted that guy for his salt block. Ruined everything. It true Yumi got a deer?"

Hunter nodded. Yumi must have heard. She looked over to Hunter and smiled.

"Yumi got a deer and you didn't." Kelton tried to muffle his laugh. "S'matter, Higgins? Too afraid? You let a girl fight your battles?"

This was what Hunter had feared more than anything back in the woods when he'd been unable to shoot the deer. But now it didn't bother him. He noticed Annette in the next row had heard Kelton. She frowned, and Hunter expected a classic Annette *Sshh*. Instead she pulled a piece of paper from her blue folder and handed it across the aisle to Kelton. She was an expert paper-passer. Miss Foudy hadn't noticed.

Hunter risked a questioning look at Annette. She only winked, and held up a copy of the newest edition of the *McCall*

Middle School Times. The headline: "Hunter Higgins Shoots Wolf, Saves Two Students." There was even a picture of Hunter covering the fallen wolf with his rifle.

"No freaking way!" Kelton Fielding whispered. "A wolf?"

Hunter, Yumi, and Annette, truly friends in the great outdoors, exchanged a look and, knowing they couldn't face worse trouble in the classroom than they had that weekend in the woods, they all three laughed.

ACKNOWLEDGMENTS

DEAR READER, IF YOU ARE ONE OF THOSE PEOPLE WHO reads the acknowledgements before reading the novel, be advised: a minor spoiler follows. Also, I hope this expression of gratitude will entice you to go back and read the book.

Through the course of this story, Hunter Higgins discovers the importance of teamwork in hunting. Fortunately, this is a lesson I learned long ago about writing. *Hunter's Choice*, like all my books, would not be possible without the help of many people. In particular, I owe special thanks:

To Mrs. Alison Foudy, a fantastic librarian at McCall-Donnelly High School, and to Jim Foudy, the district superintendent, for hosting me in McCall, Idaho, for a crucial three-day research visit. To the small army of young McCall hunters who volunteered their time to answer my many questions about the sport they love: Annette Rooney, Morgan Vawter, Jacob Coffey-Kelly, Bryden, Tannin Grant, Seth Julian, Avery Riggs, Kelton Wattace, Sam Jacobsen, Milo Papenberg, Barett Wiltinger, Oakley Palmer, McKenzie Crockett, Seth Raimert,

Jack Duncan, Wylee Onthank, Dakota Hughes, Hunter Wilcaf, Kaelin Ashley, Jordan Goodwin, Liam McCarthy, Carynn, Lavimore, and Felicia McPherson—your hunting insights were essential for writing this book.

To Nick Jeffries, Marine veteran and consummate hunter, for his advice.

To retired Army National Guard Staff Sergeant Jacob Pries for his expertise in firearms and ammunition, and for his patience with my many questions.

To my fantastic editor, Simon Boughton, for thinking of me and for trusting me with this book and series. No other book I've ever written has come together so quickly and that is in large part thanks to your expertise. It's been a lot of fun working with you, and I look forward to the books to come.

To my mother, Lu Ann, for hosting me on my trips to Iowa for author visits to schools and before my hunting trip. It's always great to see you and to get back to good old Dysart.

To my brother-in-law Travis Klima, to whom I dedicate this novel. You're a great hunter and the best brother-in-law for which a man might hope. Thank you very much for letting me walk along on your hunting adventure, for answering so many hunting and deer questions, and for test-reading this manuscript. This book wouldn't exist without you. I hope you shoot the biggest deer, wolf, or bear on record. It's prime time!

To ultra-premium agent extraordinaire Ammi-Joan Paquette, for connecting me with Mr. Boughton and the good people at Norton Young Readers, for patience in the face of my many doubts, and for endless help through the years I've been publishing books. Joan, you were my first professional YES, and you've been with me every step of the way. Thanks for a great first decade in this wild writing life.

To my daughter Verity for her patience as I worked on this book and for going with me on the research trip to McCall. I'm sorry I couldn't always play Legos or Fireball Island when you wanted, but I thank you for letting me write this book. I had fun searching for Sharlie the lake monster with you.

To my wonderful wife, Amanda, for believing in my crazy writing dream even and especially when I had my own doubts, for listening to myriad story ideas, and for tolerating an occasionally less than perfectly clean house when I was on deadline. Amanda, you are my life.

AN EXCERPT FROM
RACING STORM MOUNTAIN

ON ONE OF THE SNOWMOBILING YOUTUBE VIDEOS KELTON had watched, the pro who was offering all the riding tips started with Rule 1: Don't Forget to Breathe. Watching it, Kelton had thought it was the dumbest thing. He'd figured it was physically impossible to forget to breathe. Even an unconscious guy kept breathing.

Yet now, in the seconds before the starting pistol signaled the beginning of the race, he understood. His muscles tense, he gripped his handlebars tight, ready to blip the throttle and pour on the speed. But he wouldn't crank it full blast. Everybody else could shoot ahead into a big cluster, bumping into each other, hitting the brakes, trying to get clear. He'd let the crowd jump ahead, and then spot his way around.

With his shortcut, he didn't need to be in the lead. He was going to bypass a major portion of the racecourse. Straight through checkpoint one, up over the gold mine pass, and right down to checkpoint two ahead of everyone else. Then it would be a wide-open trail for him to speed along at a good pace, safe from anyone else's interference. In less than an hour, he'd own the coolest snowmobile in America.

The starting pistol fired, and he blipped the throttle, revving the machine up to get it going, but then hanging back for a moment while the rest of the herd surged into a giant knot of snowmobiles ahead of him.

"Breathe!" he said quietly to himself inside his helmet. "On the left!" There was a space to shoot through if he really gunned it. Kelton sped up his sled, riding for all he was worth to squeeze through the tiny, single-snowmobile space on the left side. "Come on, come on, come on!" One guy on a blue snowmobile ahead of Kelton looked like he was steering for the outside too.

"Don't do it!" Kelton shouted, even though he knew nobody could hear him through his helmet and out here in the roar from all the snowmobiles. "Come on!" He called to his own sled. "You can do it!"

With inches to spare, Kelton shot through the gap and glided into a great position in the center of the trail, just a few lengths behind the half-dozen sleds leading the race.

Now he blazed ahead, risking a quick look at the pack behind him. His snowmobile raced down the well-groomed and packed trail, flying across the white, through a sort of tunnel formed by the tree branches overhead.

It was happening! He was way out near the front, and with his super-time-saving shortcut still to come. The race was his. His sled was running great. He could feel its power, like it was hungry, tearing at the snow, the track biting solid and throwing the machine over the white faster and faster.

Kelton rode like that, mostly on a straightaway, but taking a few small curves, careful to always hug the inside of them, to take as straight a path as possible. The speed was fantastic. Several times he laughed at the delight of it all. Everything flew by in a blur, like this whole amazing day was a dream, like he'd fallen asleep on that bench seat in the garage near his snowmobile last night and at any moment he could wake up from this. But then his snowmobile would shoot up over a little bump, flipping his stomach with that split second of weightlessness, like when a roller coaster whips over a sharp hill, and he knew, more than at any other time that he was awake, and more alive than he'd ever been before.

He peered through the light mist that the lead snowmobiles kicked up in their wake. Seven, maybe eight machines ahead of him. And beyond them, barely visible, was it? Yes! Orange flags on tall poles on either side of the trail! Checkpoint one, coming up about a hundred, hundred fifty yards ahead. About a half mile after that was the turnoff trail for his shortcut.

"Maybe just stay on the main course," Kelton said inside his helmet. "You're only in ninth place or something. Maybe just ride the whole thing and try to pass them."

But even as he said it, he knew that was crap. The leaders were probably Richies on the fastest sleds out there. Hard to tell with the gear and helmets, but he was pretty sure that was Bryden Simmons on his charged Polaris up ahead. Thing is, this race, like all of life, wasn't an example of fairness. No. The shortcut was his only chance to even things out. It meant for a slightly tougher run through deeper powder, but he could do it.

He patted his snowmobile. "You ready for this?" Then suddenly he was through the first checkpoint, and watching intensely for his secret turn.

"Come on. Where are you?" Kelton said to himself. The turnoff was easy to see on the map. But maps aren't real life. No rock outcroppings on a map. On a map, the trees didn't block the view like they did in real life. His shortcut wasn't part of the county's well-maintained trail system. It might be quite overgrown, hard to spot. And there were lots of side trails off the main route. How could he know which was his shortcut? On the map, his pass wound up between the Big and Little McCall peaks, but it was hard to see the mountains down in the woods. Maybe he should have checked the distance on the map, tried to measure how far he'd gone beyond the checkpoint.

Kelton kept glancing to his right, trying to spot the high valley between the two peaks, looking for a clearing or even a trace of the road. Finally, the woods thinned out a little as the trail ran slightly closer to a distant creek. Was this it? Coming up on his right?

"It has to be." He knew he'd eventually have to risk trying one of these side trails, hoping it was the right one. If he was wrong, he'd lose the race. There would be no second chance. He could try one of the offshoots, hoping it was his shortcut, and maybe win the race.

He was tired of being the outcast, the last picked, the unseen, forgotten one. Just this once, he would finally do something right, finally get something besides the worst of everything, finally . . . *win!* He cranked his snowmobile hard to the right, leaning in that direction to center himself as he skidded through a tight turn, and an instant later he was flying ahead through much looser powder. He squeezed the throttle to give the sled the extra power it needed, and it bucked ahead over the uneven snow. Other snowmobiles had taken this path a while back, because compared to the snow on either side, the trail was kind of packed down, but this route hadn't been used since the most recent heavy snowfalls.

There was just one way to know if he'd taken the right path. A long time ago, train tracks ran up the pass to the gold mine, with a railroad bridge over a stream. The tracks and bridge were long gone, but if he was running their former path right now, there should be a little rise before the creek. These days people called it Stone Cold Gap, Kelton guessed any snowmobiler crazy enough to try to jump over the creek had to have stone-cold nerves. He slowed down as his rough trail rose up a little slope, and he hit the brakes hard, skidding to a halt, his heart leaping for a moment as he worried he was about to spill forward into the freezing stream below.

Kelton took off his helmet for just a moment, the icy sting of the winter air a welcome change from the tense heat inside his helmet. "Stone Cold Gap." He smiled. He'd found the right trail after all. Now he'd turn around, go back to give himself a running start, and then, if his courage held, he'd gun it full speed for the most intense snowmobile jump of his life.